Isaac Montgomery for the Love of Beth

Isaac Must Do What Needs to Be Done, His Life Will Depend on It

The trilogy

Steven Anthony

authorHOUSE®

AuthorHouse™ UK
1663 Liberty Drive
Bloomington, IN 47403 USA
www.authorhouse.co.uk
Phone: 0800.197.4150

Published by AuthorHouse   12/19/2016

ISBN: 978-1-5246-6815-0 (sc)
ISBN: 978-1-5246-6816-7 (hc)
ISBN: 978-1-5246-6814-3 (e)

Print information available on the last page.

From a loving husband…
Dedicated to my wife and three beautiful daughters.

CHAPTER ONE

Turbulence

OUR STORY BEGINS WITH A man named Isaac Montgomery. Born in a well-to-do family on the outskirts of London, in a district called Beaconsfield, he was the youngest of the three children. His father was a well-respected businessman in the city, dealing in stocks and commodities. He was also an MP for his borough. His mother was equally occupied. She was a member of the Women's Guild and various other committees, including coffee mornings and so on. She was also an outspoken advocate for women's rights in the workplace. Isaac's sister, Helen had become a barrister for one of the top firms of solicitors in Knightsbridge. His brother, Edward had gone into the army as an officer with merit and had now become one of the Queen's personal guards. Then there was Isaac. He attended boarding school from an early age and was used to seeing his parents maybe three times a year, depending upon where in the world they were at the time. From boarding school, Isaac went to the university for about five years, and then a flat was provided for him in the city, where he worked as a stockbroker for five years. He was very successful at his work, amassing a small fortune of his own. He was living the life of a millionaire playboy - fast cars, loose women, drinks, drugs with no real love in his life, other than making money and living the flamboyant lifestyle. At some point, however, it started to come to his attention that many within his small circle of friends were getting into long term relationships - marrying, starting families, settling down and becoming more responsible with their lives. This was completely alien to Isaac; he had never felt love and had just been looked after by his family until he could stand on his own two feet. Even now, he had minimal interactions with his family, which were only limited to weddings, funerals, and occasional lunches, if they could make the time. The women that Isaac took to clubs, restaurants, holidays, or family function, were just day or night dates; he never intended to know anything of their true nature, their likes, and dislikes, or their lives for that matter. To him, it was always more like a business transaction than a potential future relationship. His view was 'you want a good time, I need a date; we're both happy.' Unfortunately, Isaac's train of thought was gradually changing. He had started to imagine what it would be like to find that significant other in his life; someone to share the good and bad times with; to no longer just think of himself, but to care for someone special in his life. He realised that this was not going to happen anytime soon with the lifestyle that he was currently leading. Everyone thought of him as the kind who was never willing to settle down. For all, he was just an ambitious playboy, who used and abused, and then moved on. He ran on full throttle, not to be tamed by anyone. A bright star that would one day be extinguished and forgotten. Isaac's friends had also once lived their lives in the fast lane but had decided to settle down and become more responsible within their personal lives. They had found that special person to love and share companionship, to create a legacy not to be forgotten. They were no longer just chasing money until they burnt themselves out with nothing but a pot of gold to love and hold, void of companionship unless paid for. This was something that had started playing on Isaac's mind, but he was clueless as to how to move forward. So, he decided to seek the help of his friend Phillip, another high-flyer who had now settled down with a girl called Penelope, a legal secretary in the city. For Phil, it had been about an instant attraction followed by a long drawn-out pursuit, until he got his lady, and now they were very much in love and planning a future together.

When Isaac thought of love and relationships, it was his parents' marriage that always came to his mind. It was a marriage of convenience, as opposed to a life partnership situation. They both needed their space to pursue their individual careers. They had children, as it was expected to carry on the family legacy. They could put up with each other when required and it all seemed very amicable. They showed that they could both basically tolerate each other's company on the surface and find their own versions of a status quo behind closed doors. They would have separate holidays, separate lives and just keep up the facade for the public's view. As he had never really had a loving, nurturing relationship with his parents, this seemed the norm. That is the only real experience Isaac had seen and he believed that a relationship would always be like this for him. Of course, he felt attracted to women he would meet, but this was more to suit his lifestyle. He had never really needed a full-time partner and he had never before really given it any thought, but now as he was reaching his thirtieth year. The thought of settling down and perhaps meeting that special someone, who could bring fulfillment to his life, began to slowly creep up on him. Although Isaac was very fortunate in his business where money making was concerned, he was finding himself growing weary of his chosen profession and craved change. In his material world, the cut and thrust no longer interested him. He had spent ten years relentlessly chasing money with very little ethics or concerns on how he obtained it or who he had to crush, destroy, belittle or betray in the process. Lives fell apart around him, other people's lives. But this would just fill him with a frenzied excitement of one-upmanship and the best of the best. May God help anyone who got in his way! Isaac was finally at the stage, where money seemed secondary to the quest for finding meaning and purpose, and perhaps this thing called love that he never truly understood. Isaac hesitantly walked towards Phillip's apartment in Kensington wondering, "How do I ask somebody, especially another man, about love and feelings, without sounding gay? I have just never cared for how people would be affected by my actions." Isaac had a new appreciation for emotion, which seemed to fill his mind at night when he was trying to sleep. He thought this must be compassion, accelerating to guilt? Would it be possible that any woman would want to live or love somebody, who is so empty, arrogant and shallow as he had become? Isaac had realised that he would have to change before he loses himself with not a shred of humanity left. He did not want to become just a husk of a man; living alone in a big house with pots of money and no will to live, having spent every waking moment of his miserable time in this world pushing people away because he could not connect. As Isaac arrived at Phillip's door, he rang the doorbell and waited. There was no reply, so he rang again. The door slowly opened and a pair of beady eyes popped out. "Oh, it's you?" Phil said. "Well, you better come in then. I'm having an occasional day at home." Phil stood there in his baggy tracksuit bottoms and a badly creased sweatshirt, one slipper on, the other presumably having escaped the stench of his feet. Phil was always impeccably dressed. In fact, Isaac thought when Phil was born, he must have come out wearing a suit and designer Italian shoes. "Have you lost your job?" Isaac asked, "...or blown a deal on the stock market?"

"No," he replied, "I'm just having, what we call a slop day. That's when I don't bother getting dressed or washed; I just totally chill out and do nothing, except what I want to do. Pen said it would help me to de-stress and set me up for the next day's trading, and guess what...it really works! After a day like this, I feel totally relaxed and ready for the early morning onslaught in the stock exchange. Anyways, enough about me... what brings you here? No bad news, I hope? That will spoil my slop day. I think this is the second time you have been here in the past year. In fact, I was beginning to think you were a figment of my imagination, it has been so long. You're still going to be my best man, I hope? Or are you going to mess that up as well?"

Isaac replied, "If you let me speak something, I will tell you why I am here... it's for your help and experience."

Phil replied, "Oh, so what...are you admitting that I am a better stockbroker than you and you need my help because you know I reign supreme!"

"Well," Isaac chuckled, "I love the fact that you have a good imagination. I waste more money than you make, you're my bitch! No... joking apart, I don't quite know how to go about this... but it's like this, um...well...I...how can I say it? Oh, for God's sake...how to go about having a relationship with a woman or know if she is the one or not? How do you know when you fall in love? What is it like? What are the feelings that you are supposed to have? How do you know if she feels the same? Basically, how do you put up with a long-term relationship?" Isaac looked at Phil, who was completely amazed. It looked as if somebody had just died in front of him. Isaac quickly said, "Well, give me the short version, because I have got a busy day planned and I need to get back to the office. I am expecting some important calls from the clients in China and India. So, you have about 30 minutes of my valuable time. If I don't get the right answers, I will have to bill you for half a day, which means you will have to give me the keys to your apartment and just owe me the rest."

Phil sat there looking at Isaac, with a surprised expression on his face, as if Isaac had just squeezed his privates or pinched his Lamborghini. Phil eventually replied, "Well... where do I start? You have given me 30 minutes to explain one of the life's greatest mysteries - 'What is love?' It will take me 30 minutes to just think of what I can say, and that would just start with love is... and that would be my stumbling block...!"

"Come on, time is money," Isaac prompted.

"Ok here it goes, when you were a child, you loved your mother and father, right?"

"Well, no," Isaac replied. "I can't remember that feeling for them, because, from my earliest recollection of family life, I had a nanny and my parents were just strange faces, I would see from time to time. On the plus side, I did learn to speak Portuguese quite fluently. As my brother and sister were a lot older than me, they had already gone to the boarding school and were busy with other things, so I never felt any bonding with them. At the time, I didn't even know they existed. I could have been an only child, for all I knew. I was just a mistake as I found out much later. So, no I didn't feel love as you call it, I just felt kept; like a well-trained pet with a very good education. Don't get me wrong, I never went without anything I desired; whatever I needed was always provided for. I had good friends and supportive teachers, so in a lot of ways this was my life and I knew no different. I never thought I had missed out on anything, until now. I suppose I never understood love because I don't think I have ever felt any. I like some people, but I am not put out if I don't see them for a long time, I just get on with other things. Life has always been for living and doing whatever you want. But somehow, now, that is not enough, I feel something is missing and I need to know what that is. Tell me how and why you fell for Penelope."

Phil paused for a moment, as if recalling the memory, and then replied, "Well that's as good a place to start as any. Do you remember last November 17th - we had bought gold, as the market started to fall with the forthcoming onslaught of the credit crunch. Remember, we bought low and suddenly there was a surge of people investing in gold. That was one of the best days of my life; we made millions for ourselves and our company. After that, we had gone to that wine bar, near Charring Cross. It was there when I first saw Pen. She was standing with a few friends at the bar and I just knew. Don't you remember, I said to you, 'That's the girl I will marry one day'? Do you recollect? You said that I had drunk too much and I was gay and you can push your own stool in. All that night, all I could do was just stare at her, imagining a life with her; our house, children, cars, etc. A fairy-tale world, where anything was possible. We would never argue, and always be best friends. Our love would last an eternity. Now come to think about it, I must have been pretty drunk. I didn't even introduce myself to her. Though I really don't think I was sober enough to string my sentences together. However, I do remember my face being pressed against the pavement. I must have dropped something... my dignity!" Phil chuckled and continued "Anyway, for weeks after that night I kept missing the boys' night outs and would make my way to that wine bar, where I first saw Pen, but it seemed almost like she would never cross my path again. After months of waiting for a glimpse of her, I realised that it was not to be and reluctantly had to admit defeat. At this time I didn't even know her name or where she worked. In fact, nothing about her, but the fact that I thought I loved her and wanted to get married to her to be together forever! There was no rhyme or reason to the way I felt. Anyways, a couple of months went by and she was slowly pushed to the back of my mind. I thought it was not meant to be. Then one fateful day, I had to go to Whitechapel for a business meeting. I was strolling along, with not a care in the world, and I happened to see Pen. There she was, visible through the window of a coffee shop. She looked lost as if her mind was somewhere else. I was frozen to the spot."

Isaac was getting impatient with this emotional banter. He interrupted, "I've got to say you are boring me now, can we cut to the chase?"

Phillip exclaimed, "If you want to hear about my experiences, shut your gob and listen! I don't know why you think any woman would want you, you arrogant shit. She would be better off with a Labrador!"

"Ok, message received and understood. Please continue. I'm sorry. I was just trying to stop you from breaking into tears, you wuss," Isaac joked.

"Well thanks for that, you unfeeling twat! I will continue with my story of a real man's life of love and commitment. As I said, I was frozen on the spot. A million questions were zooming through my head - Should

I go in, or stay out? Is my hair alright? Does my breath smell? What if she ignores me? What should I say? My meeting was in about ten minutes and I still needed five to get there. No, I thought, this is too important, so I manned up and walked straight up to her and said, 'Hello again, do you remember me from the wine bar in Charring Cross? You were there with a few friends; I was there with a few work colleagues, just celebrating our success that day on the stock market'. Penelope was totally confused and said, 'No, I can't say that I remember you. Did we talk or bump into each other?' I tried to make her remember, 'Well, I sat right opposite to where you were talking with your friends. I really wanted to ask you out, but I couldn't gather the courage. So I just sat there giving you my best puppy dog eyes, hoping that you would take pity on me and come across.' Finally, she said, 'Now I remember! Aren't you the one who was kissing the pavement outside? And now that you mention it, I do remember you looking at me constantly. I remember thinking you were special – but not in a good way. But now that you are standing in front of me, I must say you scrub up well.' She was giggling. I still remember how her eyes were shining at that time. I wanted to spend a few more minutes with her, so I said, 'Why do people always remember the bad things you do?' She replied with a wink, 'Well, I suppose it is probably because I don't know the good things yet.' I knew this meant that we connected and I immediately asked her out on the spot, and she agreed and the rest is history. I suppose love was that initial spark, that feeling, me imagining all those different scenarios, showing me a future that I had never even thought of. Suddenly, I wanted to be with that other person. From that one spark, our relationship grew to where it is today and I can't imagine my life without her anymore. There is not one thing I would change about her, and I want so much to get married, settle down and perhaps have children. And I do not want either work or life to devalue what we have."

He continued, "So in answer to the question you asked – what is love? – Well, I think it means different to different people, from friendship to an attraction. Perhaps the way one person perceives another, companionship, a need to love and be loved, to be there for each other through the good times and the bad. A lot of people search all of their lives for that, from partner to partner, never truly finding the person that they want and as a result, never finding fulfillment in their lives. This is just the way I perceive love personally. I think you should seek help from somebody, who can explain it to you better than me, and while you are there, perhaps they could cure your attitude you self-righteous bastard!" Phil concluded. Isaac did not respond, just sat in silence for a few moments. "Well... are you going to say something?" Phil gestured at Isaac.

Isaac answered, "Well, to be honest, it is a foreign concept to me. I really don't know what to say. I thank you for your honesty and I do think you put your analogies across most eloquently, but these are the feelings that I have never really experienced before. Does that mean I am incapable of finding that certain person because I would not recognize her even if she was standing before me? And more so, would I be able to give her the love and commitment that makes these sort of bonding relationships? Well at this moment, it doesn't seem so. These feelings are way too complicated - thinking about someone else and not the job at hand, consideration for each other, having to discuss and not just do. I work hard and I play hard, my personal life is uncomplicated. I eat where I want, I drink where I want and whatever I do, I do it for me. If I want a date, I just pick up the phone; we have a night out followed by sex and the way I want it. They leave in the morning, I go to work, and it all starts over again. Nobody gets hurt and we both have a good time!"

Phil interrupted, "But do they have a good night or do you just think they did because you had a good time? You are so selfish and self-centered that you only think of yourself. Did you actually stop for a minute and asked her how she felt or did you just take her for granted? At some time during the night, did you take a moment to actually have a dialogue with the poor girl and ask her how her day had been, if everything was ok in her life, did she like the club you had brought her to? No, of course, you didn't. You just partied the night away and if she was there at the end of the night, she was going to get lucky. You are so arrogant, it all has to be about you. Nothing else matters and to be honest I don't think that you deserve someone special to care about you because you will rip out her heart and stomp on it, and then will just move on to your next victim. I just don't think I am the right person to help you and now you have made me explain my feelings. You must want something before you can find it and I am not really sure that you are grown-up enough to find what you are looking for. Your best bet would be to find someone just like yourself and you can become your mother and father all over again and bring another unwanted demon into the world."

There was complete silence. Phil asked, "Has anything I have said actually gone into that thick skull of yours, or would I have been better talking to the wall? If you knew what you wanted to do and be, then why ask for my advice? My answer to your question is that you are a bloody Vulcan…now live with it!"

Isaac sat bewildered for a moment and then responded, "You know, nobody has ever spoken to me like that, and if it was anybody else but you, I would have twatted them, but I have known you since the university days. And trust me, I do take what you have said seriously. This is because I have never seen you so passionate about any other subject or question before. I have to ask, is that really what I come across to you as and others in life? Am I that shallow that I just couldn't see it? It is as though my whole life has been a fantasy of my own making. I am beginning to feel so guilty for the way I have treated people over the years. I want to thank you for never giving up on me. I do want to change, I do want to be a better person, and most of all I don't want to be alone! But how, how can I change the life I have been given and raised up to? How do I make that stop?" Isaac looked confused, with a hint of desperation.

Phil looked concerned and answered, "I think you must stop living your life the way that you are used to. You have more than enough money to last you a lifetime. Get away from everything you have known all your life and find a new way to experience people and the beauty around you. You have been so involved in trying to prove yourself as the best at whatever you do that you've never really taken the time to see the world around you and to experience the smallest things that make life worthwhile. Things like a summer's day in the country, a baby being born, the rustle of the leaves before a storm, the wonders of a winter snow as it blankets the ground around you and the sounds of silence when you make peace with who you are and who you want to be. The chase that you have pursued so long must end now if you want to find love. First, you must find yourself because that is where your journey begins. You must learn to love life, appreciate what life is - the sky, the wind, the forests, the oceans. Meet with people, talk to them, take an interest in what you hear, ask questions, debate, take time out to do things you would like to try, fishing or boating or whatever it is, and these are only the examples of what you could do with your life. Read romantic books, see how others have found love in their lives, write your feelings down in a diary and see how the pages grow as the time goes on. Slowly, you'll find love for the things around you and one day you will be able to answer your question yourself, 'What is love?'"

Isaac was just shocked with the realisation of his own feelings. He said, "I cannot believe the things you have just said to me. Where is the Philip I knew, what have you done with him? What you said actually made sense to me. It was as if a door that I have tried to get into all of my life has been opened. I used to feel that I was broken in some way, and nobody could repair me. But the truth is only I can undo what has been done and I can do that by opening my eyes and focusing on myself for a change, instead of living and breathing the chase to make more and more money with no regards for anyone, but myself. I agree that I never had the childhood of loving relationship with my parents and I never grew up like other children did, but I always got all the material things that I wanted. I did have friends and teachers, who cared for me and encouraged me to do well. As I pursued my career, I forgot just what I did have growing up. In my arrogance, I sought no help from anyone. I achieved everything myself against all the odds, and the only one that mattered in my world was me. What a fool I have been!"

Philip asked, "So, where do you go from here, Isaac?"

"I must admit I don't know! I have got a lot of soul searching to do. I asked you to explain love and caring to me, and my God you did it. I do ask myself when was the last time we sat like this, as friends, and really discussed anything of importance or put the world to rights," Isaac said, looking at Philip.

Philip looked back at Isaac and remembered, "We actually used to do it quite often at the uni. Sometimes such conversations turned out to be all-nighters, but once we left uni and you started your new job, it became less and less frequent, until eventually, it stopped altogether. For you, it became all about your career and making money, being seen at the top places, always with a beautiful woman on your arm. Fast cars, designer everything. You went from being a half decent bloke to a money monster. You never wanted to talk about life, because you knew everything; you had become a self-righteous Frigg."

Isaac sat with a look of total disbelief on his face, taking everything in that his friend was saying. He was fighting back the tears, as they suddenly began to swell up in his eyes, and gently began to flow down his cheek. He was trying to use all his willpower to stop it, but to no avail. In his own mind he was thinking, "I have never cried, no matter what," but now they were beginning to flow like a mountain stream. He just broke down, completely inconsolable. Thirty years of keeping all of his emotions in check, never showing weakness, to now uncontrollably releasing his innermost feelings out into the world. His lips were quivering, his speech was broken, he was fighting to stop himself, but everything that he had repressed had now pushed itself through to rush into his mind to show him just how much of life he had really missed. There would be no consoling him until his epiphany had subsided.

Philip could not believe his eyes; an ego as big as Isaac's was brought down by the word 'love'. He was suddenly realising just how repressed his friend had become as a result of never really knowing love. He had never seen any compassion as a boy. To his parents, he was probably just the mistake that they had to live with. He did everything to show them that he existed as he wanted to be their son. Isaac would have to come to terms with all this and realise that nothing was his fault. His life had driven him down to this path because he wanted love from the people that had brought him into this world, he just didn't know what had been missing from his life, but now his emotions were running rampant and showing him a slideshow of the things that he had somehow forgotten.

Philip pondered to himself, for now, he could not reach Isaac. "I hope he hasn't had a nervous breakdown, that isn't what I wanted. I just want him to live and to know there is a life out there, other than the self-destructive one he has been living. I will wait until he calms down and then perhaps find out what he wants to do…or should I call an ambulance?"

CHAPTER TWO

Transformation

A COUPLE OF HOURS WENT by. Philip dawdled, as Isaac huddled on the sofa, just mumbling to himself. From time to time, Philip popped his head around the kitchen door, just to check on his friend and found that he had drifted off to sleep, cuddling a pillow. Philip was very worried. He had already sent a panic message to Pen. He had never seen Isaac so vulnerable and lost. Philip said to himself, "Am I responsible for this condition, did I push him too far? I must phone Penelope and ask her to come home immediately. I just don't know what to do. And if he wakes up, what do I say, 'Sorry'? He asked me a question and I gave him my version of an answer. I told him he needed to speak to someone else. Somebody trained in this sort of thing." Irrespective of what he said, Philip could not get rid of that guilty feeling.

Phillip said to himself, "Come on you prat, wake up and tell me that everything is ok!"

Just then there was a sound of a key in the front door as if someone was hastily trying to get in. Phil ran to the door. It was Penelope. She had raced back home, after Philip's frantic message on the mobile - "Get home quick….something's happened to Isaac!" Pen didn't know if there had been an accident or what, just the voice of panic on the other end of the line.

Pen burst in, looked around to survey the situation and barked, "Right, what has happened?"

Phil raced to tell Pen as he got his words all muddled in an incoherent babble. The only word she could understand were, "It's not my fault."

"Stop. Take a deep breath and tell me what has happened. We'll go into the kitchen and you take your own time to explain what's wrong, while I make us a nice cup of tea."

Phil started to explain, "I was just having a nice chilled out day like you said I needed. The next thing I knew, there was a knock at the door. I wondered whether I should answer it or pretend that no one is in. Anyways, someone knocked again, so I had to see who it was. To my surprise, Isaac was stood there and it was a work day. He asked if he could have a chat. There was something he had to ask me, so I asked him in. He needed advice about something that had been playing on his mind..." Philip then went on to explain all that had transpired between him and Isaac, till he reached the part of Isaac's breakdown or whatever it was.

"I kept checking on him, but he fell asleep. He has been sleeping for hours, but there is no sign of him waking up anytime soon. Should I try to wake him up?"

Pen sighed and shook her head. "No, leave him alone. Shutting down like he has is probably just what his body has told him he needs. When he wakes, he may see things in a new light – or he'll punch you in the face, from what you have told me. If I was you I would go and look for a hockey mask! Why couldn't he come to me or another woman for advice on love? He definitely should not have come to a man who has only just realised what he has in his life, after years of self-indulgence."

Phil looked upset as if disappointed. "Oh, don't you have a go at me. I was just trying to be a good friend. I threw a few digs along the way, but the last thing I thought was that he would have a breakdown!"

Pen's tone lowered. "Well let's not get ahead of ourselves. We don't know if he has had a breakdown or if his tiredness has just caught up with him. You have said yourself that he burns the candle at both ends and never seems to sleep anymore. And by the way he is dressed, it looks like he has just come straight from a club. Let's just wait. You are a numpty sometimes! If I didn't love you, I would kick you in the ass between here and London Bridge."

"But you do love me, don't you Pen?" Phil inquired in a childlike voice.

"Well, if you don't even know that, then why in the world, were you giving advice to someone else about love? Is it because you think you have all of the answers where love is concerned or you just don't think it through? Again I will say…you numpty!" Pen said raising her eyebrows.

Philip and Pen carried on with their heated discussion, only pausing to eat for a moment, then Penny shared her interpretation of love and marriage with Phil. Being one with each other, Phil realised that Penny knew a lot more about relationships than he ever thought possible. She told him about once getting engaged to a man, she thought she really loved. But she later realised that he never wanted the same things in life as she did. In fact, in his own words, he bought her a ring to just keep her off his back about commitment as he never really wanted to marry her. This conversation went on till the middle of the night until they were both too tired to talk anymore.

Unbelievably, what had happened with Isaac, had finally allowed them to open up with each other and share stories of the past and their lives. This helped them discuss all of the good and bad experiences they went through; it was all out in the open. There was nothing to hide, there was only the truth, the sort of truth that binds people together forever. They had experienced what they needed in their lives and now they had found each other and that is what mattered the most. Phil and Pen finally decided to seal the night with a night of passion. This time with a renewed height of sensitivity and longing for the night to never end. The stories they had shared had resulted in an enhanced acceleration of their feelings towards each other. It had awakened their desires in special little ways with which they liked to touch and caress. They had realised that they always wanted to be together. Their eyes were open and they saw each other for who they were; no hidden agendas and no longing for anything else. They would make it last and count their blessings, they were meant to be. The universe had chosen them to be together.

As they stumbled across the apartment, in love's embrace, bumping into everything like drunken monkeys, they suddenly realised that Isaac was sleeping soundly on the sofa.

It suddenly dawned on Pen. "What about Isaac? We can't just leave him here. What if there is something wrong with him and we are engrossed in the bedroom?"

"Oh, he will be alright! Get thee hence to the bedroom wench!" Phil stumbled as he tried to caress Penelope's body.

Pen tried to move away from him a little and replied, "Oh that's it, you cause the problem and as usual I have to sort it out. We'll have to put it off until tomorrow."

Phil's face dropped as he moaned, "Oh come on…I'm being a good boy and I am already standing to attention. Do you want to see? Would you like to admire my manhood?" Phil said as he looked down with a proud grin.

"If you are so shallow about your friend's predicament, go to the bathroom and give yourself a tug. That's something I know you can do. I've seen your special sock that you think you have so cleverly hidden under the mattress in the bedroom."

"Well, I am just saying that he is sound asleep and we are all hot and wet. How about a quickie?" Philip said in his playful tone.

Pen was serious, "So, what you are saying is that you want a quickie for yourself so that you can just empty your tank…as you call it? Nothing for me, but just a mess to clean up! I really thought you were becoming sensitive to a woman's needs and then you revert to Neanderthal man. Just do what you have to do and get back here. We will take turns to watch Isaac through the night."

"I'll go to the bathroom then," Phil reluctantly said, as he walked off.

"Get back here, you dirty little bastard. I didn't think for a minute that you would really do it! After everything we talked about for hours, you go and totally astound me with the revelation that I'm in love with a wanker!" Pen said in a gruff tone.

"I'm sorry I was only joking…I wouldn't have really done it," Phil said sheepishly.

"Oh yes, you would have!" Pen added.

Phil's expression changed as he realised Pen was becoming more serious. "I am sorry. I was being inconsiderate of your feelings and I do apologise. I meant everything I said and I do love you more than I can possibly put into words. I suppose it's going to take a little time for me to get out of the habit of being a dickhead, but I endeavour to do that!"

"I will hold you to that and don't you forget it! Right, you go off to bed and I will take first watch over Isaac. I will wake you in about 4 hours and if he is not awake by then, you can watch him," Pen said, the smile returning to her face.

"Can I have a kiss?" Phil hesitantly asked.

Penelope's serious tone returned. "No, I am too angry with you at the moment, so just go to bed! I will be checking your sock later, so don't you-know-what in our bed."

"Goodnight Pen, love you. Do you love me?" Phil murmured.

"Just go to bed!" Pen snapped.

Penelope settled herself down on the over-sized armchair, they kept especially for chilled out days. It was big and comfy and full of feathers. Wrapping herself nicely and snugly in a blanket, she sat vigil over Isaac. She tried not to let her mind wander about what Isaac would possibly be like when he wakes up in the morning. The night moved swiftly as if racing towards an answer to the question, "What will be?" Pen didn't wake Philip; he had to be at work early the next day and would need a full night's sleep. He needed his wits about him in his profession, whereas she could take an occasional day off for herself and catch up with her sleep during the day. She sat reading a book, only getting up occasionally to make a cup of coffee or use the loo. Sometime during the night she must have drifted off into a waking sleep, where you think you are awake but are actually in a semi-coma. Bearing in mind the trauma of the day before, she suddenly awoke totally disorientated. It was around 8.30 am in the morning. Philip had softly crept through earlier, so as not to wake her up; she looked so peaceful all wrapped up in her snuggly blanket and sleeping soundly. As she gathered her wits about her, she realised that Isaac was missing from the sofa. "Oh my God, what has happened?" she gasped. "Where the hell is he?" She jumped up, still in a partial daze, and not fully awake. There were sounds emanating from the kitchen. She could hear the sound of the kettle boiling, the rustle of spoons and drawers opening and closing, then a voice rang out; it was Isaac.

"Hello, sleepyhead! Would you like a cuppa?" There he was, bold as brass. "I hope you don't mind, I have just put some toast in and I am making a drink. I woke up suddenly when I heard Philip leave for work. You looked so comfortable that I thought I would tiptoe around to get a libation and some toast on the go," Isaac continued.

"How do you feel? We thought you had had a nervous breakdown or something. Phil told me you were in a terrible state and he just didn't know what to do with you. There was absolutely no consoling you. Then the next time he returned to the living room, you were fast asleep. Do you even know that you have been asleep for almost 16 hours? I was expecting that I would have to call the psychiatric department at the hospital this morning to tell them to just come and pick you up. But look at you, it looks like you haven't got a care in the world," Pen said through a yawn.

Isaac replied, "Well to be honest with you, I'm about to embark on a new adventure. I am going to throw away the ties of my past and start a new life! It sounds like a cliché, but I really am going to find out who I am and what I want to do with my life. For so long, I have felt that there is a void in my life and I need to find out what that is. As implausible as it may sound, it was Philip, who really opened my eyes to an alternative lifestyle. I am going to find somebody to love and be more than what I am. It was almost as if a heavy weight was being lifted, releasing all of my suppressed feelings of not being wanted as a child. My life had become nothing more than a money-making mission and I even side-stepped my happiness for my career, excelling at being a total bastard to everybody I met. How you and Phil have put up with me for so long, I have no clue. I have the morals of a gutter rat and I cared nothing for anyone. I must have been the devil incarnate. If I was to go to every person I have hurt, it would take me two lifetimes and then some more. I can't put the past right, but I can live a better life in the future or die trying. All the things I felt were important to me were a lie. I now want to live and experience life first hand!"

Pen again looked concerned as she asked, "Are you sure about this? It seems very quick. Shouldn't you take a little time to think it through? Perhaps talk to a professional and make sure you are not throwing everything away on a whim. I really hope you do not find yourself back here in six months or so wishing you hadn't been so impetuous in your decision. Give yourself time to come to terms with what you really want and need."

Isaac strongly replied, "I have. I am one of those people that fly by the seat of my pants. I make a decision and I act on it! If my so-called father ever taught me anything, it was to consider your first decision as the right decision. So for me, from now on, I will leave everything to chance and take it as it comes."

"I must admit I have never really liked you because everything always had to be about you and Philip would follow you like the good little puppy dog. You would say jump…and he would say how high? It took me a long time to break him away from your influence. There were times when I hated you, as for a while it was one step forward and two steps back with Philip. But then you lost interest, so I finally found the break I needed to get him away from you and I blamed you a lot for all that. You used to pick him up and throw him away, whenever it took your fancy, and he just followed while you led. But now, if I come to think of it, you were the lost little boy in the sweet shop being swamped by so many goodies at one time that you never knew what you wanted. You wanted it all, but you could only choose one thing and that is how you led your life. And if this decision that you have made is what you really want to do, I sincerely wish you all the best and I hope you find what you are looking for!" Pen said with a smile.

Isaac looked shocked, but was reassured, "That really means a lot to me Pen, and thank you for your honesty. I can't argue against your logic, nor would I try to. I know I have hurt many people, and I shouldn't expect anything else, but what has really surprised me is that I did all of that to you and you still sat up all night watching over me with a genuine concern for my well-being. I thank you very much for that. I have caused you so much pain in your life and you have shown me nothing but compassion and real kindness, setting your dislike to one side. I think you are one of those genuine people I am going to look for and surround my life with."

"Well, the type of person I am seeing before me right now, I would also like to know him better. So, go ahead and find your life Isaac Montgomery and we will see you at the wedding in May. I will call you to confirm!" Pen said with a cheeky smile and a raised eyebrow.

"Oh, I will be there and that is a promise! Thanks again Pen. Please tell Philip I will call him later when my mind gets a bit settled and I know where I am going. I will keep calling you guys from time to time to let you both know how I am doing. You and Philip are really great together. I will see you soon, Pen."

CHAPTER THREE

The Adventure Begins...

Now that Isaac had made up his mind, nothing could stop him. It was a Friday morning and for him, it would be a new world to explore; the beginning of a new life. The first thing he decided to do was call Mr. Van Horn, his boss, and mentor. He decided to tell him that he is overwhelmed by the events that had occurred in his personal life and would need some time off to get himself back to where he needs to be. He had been due to become a partner on the following Monday morning, and his contracts had already been drawn up and were all ready to be signed. He explained, without going into too much detail that he needed this time as in his current condition he would be useless to the company. Mr. Van Horn reluctantly agreed to sanction this time-off, presuming that it would only be a short break. But, he also knew that a stockbroker with problems in his life could cost the company a considerable amount of money in short time and that was a situation he would not consider a simple mistake. He would make sure that the perpetrator dearly pays for such an error. In the past, he had destroyed people who had made such mistakes on the stock market, leaving them with nothing but a cardboard box to live in. Isaac had seen this first hand. There are no real words to describe the shell of the human being that is left to rot in the gutter; he knows that there would never be a reprieve from their new life, because once you've lost or taken the money from the Van Horns, your life is over! In fact, several people Isaac knew had taken their own lives instead of facing the wrath of Van Horn. This was the man Isaac would have become a carbon copy of if he hadn't left now. This was what frightened him more than anything. He was already half way there and it would have only been a matter of time before he would have completely metamorphosed into Isaac Van Horn. On that day, his soul would have left his body and he would have taken up his role as the devil's advocate.

Van Horn treated him like a son, the "golden child" as he called him; he could never commit a mistake in his eyes. As mentioned before, Isaac had led a charmed life, as far as business was concerned. Everything he touched seemed to turn into gold. But of course, everything changes, nothing ever stays the same and eventually his luck would have run out. So, he considered himself lucky to be getting out before he had to face the inevitable revenge of the Van Horns. At least this way if he ever tracked him down, he could say he had had a nervous breakdown from the stress. He was in such a high-powered position that if he cannot keep figures in his head, he would break into a sweat and his nerves would shoot to pieces. Once Van Horn realised that he had nothing to offer, he would just move on to his next prodigy – at least that is the way Isaac hoped it would play out, but only time would tell. This was Isaac's chance and he was not going to give it up. He wished Van Horn the best, hoped that he didn't feel bad for the events that had arisen, and said that as soon as he felt ready to come back, he will be the first to know.

Next, Isaac called his solicitor to tell him about his plans of taking a break for an indefinite time, or until he had sorted his life out. He never gave away the fact that he may never come back to his own personal hell - London. His solicitor would arrange for renting out Isaac's Mayfair apartment on a short-term contract until he is directed differently. In fact, Isaac spent most of that day getting his affairs in order, telling friends and associates that he was not well and needed to get away for his health. He had no doubt that speculation would be rife on why he was really leaving, but that didn't bother him. People would make up their own stories and conclusions and then they would forget that Isaac Montgomery ever existed. That's London for you…yesterday's news!

The one thing Isaac pondered on a great deal was where he would want to disappear to. It was interesting to make all these plans for his new life; there was the entire world out there to explore. He was most definitely a frequent flyer with his job and had traveled quietly extensively. He had visited many places over the time but had probably never really experienced any. He sat thinking for hours, trying to remember all the places he had been to, all the things that he had liked about the country, and if he would like to visit it again. Every place reminded him of his past life, which he was trying to get away from. One of the places he had never even thought of going to was the Highlands of Scotland. The countryside was supposed to be spectacular and breathtaking in the winter. The thing was that he had never really taken the time to see what was right in front of him; he was just all about the nightlife and fast living. But this is what that had brought him to where he was now, with loads of money, but a distinct absence of love. So the decision was made - the Highlands it would be! That is where he would begin his journey. Isaac booked his flight. He would go from London to Glasgow, pick up a hire car and go to a place he had googled - the Corngurn.

It was a village right on the coast of the Scottish Highlands. From the pictures he had seen, it looked like a medium sized village with a beautifully landscaped harbour. There was a small fishing industry, but it was extensively a large farming community, with lots of sheep and cattle. But during the summer months, it catered to holiday makers, who wanted to walk, fish or just look for a quiet place to stay. With breathtaking scenes of the mountains and valleys, it also provided panoramic of the sea. It sounded just like the mini paradise that Isaac was looking for, where he could disappear from the hustle and bustle he had been so used to. It seemed like a place, where he could appreciate the real time to himself and plan for his new future, while perhaps gaining a new perspective towards life. The only fear was that the silence doesn't send him into madness. For now, he would be in the realms of the unknown. He would be going on his first adventure, the first of many he hoped. In some ways, he couldn't help remembering all the things he had done before he had the epiphany on that faithful day. He was still frightened and hesitant on beginning this journey. Was he doing the right thing? Would he be throwing everything away - his sense of achievement and all he had worked so hard for - schooling, university, and working up from the bottom at Van Horns to almost becoming a partner in a multi-billion pound company? Of course, he was scared, he was trying to change every single aspect of himself to what he hoped would be for better, and for a more fulfilled future for himself. He could see that he was living his life as a money machine, believing that anything he wanted could be bought...including love and happiness. It had been proven that it is very difficult to have both, and also quite rare.

***

After what seemed like a lifetime at the airport, Isaac's flight was announced. Still, his mind was muddled with numerous questions - "Shall I go? Is it too late for me to return to my life the way that it was? Have I planned ahead? Is it too random? What the fuck am I doing?" Then, suddenly there was an announcement over the speakers, "Can Mr. Isaac Montgomery please make his way to Gate 3, as the plane is now boarding."

That was it. For somebody whose life revolved around pressure and being able to keep his head while others were falling apart around him, today he found himself totally falling apart. Suddenly dazed and confused, it seemed to take every ounce of Isaac's willpower to reach the boarding gate. Deep down he knew that he was doing the right thing, but for the first time that he could remember, he felt really frightened and his memories of what he wanted seemed to disappear into a world of panic and confusion. He suddenly realised that throughout his life, he had always delegated work on others, he always had people to rely on, talk to, blame or just make his job easier, but now he would have no one but himself. He felt that, to the outside world, he must have seemed like a total idiot, as he tried to find his seat on the plane, walking up and down the aisle looking for his number that had completely vanished from his head. Then one of the flight stewardesses asked, "Can I help you, sir?"

Isaac explained that he cannot remember where he had to sit.

"Just show me your ticket please, sir and we will get you to the right seat," the stewardess said with a reassuring smile, as Isaac followed her. "There you go sir, seat B14. Don't worry," the stewardess explained, "everyone gets a bit nervous on their first flight."

Isaac tried to tell her that this was not his first flight, but the words just came out like a jumbled mess. He had never experienced emotions like this before; maybe this was the early stage of a real nervous breakdown. Perhaps, he should have actually spoken to a professional like Pen had suggested.

He nervously sat there. As soon as he had put on his seat belt, everything went blank. The next thing he knew was that the stewardess was waking him up. "We've arrived at Glasgow Airport, sir, and we need you to disembark the plane." He seemed to have slept more in the last few days as compared to the past few years. But, now he was fully awake and he felt once more inspired to continue with his journey.

Isaac went straight to the hire company and took possession of his car. He set the Sat Nav for the Highland village of Corngurn. As he drove, mile after mile, through various towns and villages, he suddenly found himself in the open countryside of endless winding roads. For the first time, he actually realised how beautiful and serene the countryside around him really was. The series of endless mountains and valleys and the crystal clear waters of the succession of lakes doubled the reflections of the sheer awesomeness. He realised just how insignificant we really are. Life goes on and it is how you choose to live it that makes the difference to how you are perceived. Isaac's memory was awash with the sights he saw before him. He had never before in his life taken the time to notice his surroundings and had always taken such things for granted. He had been so engrossed in his own life that he had missed so much of what life had to offer. He was now driving through blurred vision, as once again for the second time in his life, he had an uncontrollable desire to cry. Seeing such unimaginable sights with his own eyes, instead of some celluloid version, had released all of the innermost suppressed feelings. This was a chance at life that he needed so desperately. He felt this to be meaningful as he slowly started to see how empty and hollow he had become living in a city. He really never saw the wood for the trees as he had been blinded by his own success. If he hadn't taken such a radical step, at this juncture, he would have passed through his life without discovering this beauty. Isaac was feeling that he was gradually turning into a human once again and was no longer just an unfeeling, functioning robot that he had become. All of a sudden, there it was - a sign for Corngurn Village; 10 miles to go. It seemed as if he had just left Glasgow and now he was already arriving at his destination.

Thirty minutes later, Isaac reached the village. He really did not notice much, he was just looking for 'Mrs. McDougal's B&B,' which was presumably right in the middle of the village. By now, it was starting to get quite dark. Isaac remembered Mrs. McDougal saying that it was right opposite a pub called 'The Dipping Tank,' and he soon found the pub and the B&B. It was sort of double terraced house, built in a grey rock effect. It didn't even look big enough to house a small family, never mind the guests. Isaac parked directly in front of the property and hoped that there were no restrictions. Isaac rang the doorbell and the door was opened by a woman. Isaac presumed that she was Mrs. McDougal. Isaac asked her if this was the right place and she replied, "Yes, and you must be Mr. Montgomery? I was expecting you by 6 o'clock, it is now 7? I would request that in future if you fix a time, please ensure that you stick to it. I don't like to be kept waiting," she said as she turned and walked towards the desk.

Isaac thought, "Well, that's a great start, isn't it?"

"You're in room 3 at the top of the stairs. If you require breakfast, it is served between 7 am to 8.30 am. If you are late, do not expect anything, I am not here to just wait on you." Isaac finished the check-in formalities and made his way up the stairs, dragging his suitcase behind him. He, for a moment considered saying, "Well no porter, then?", but thought that it would probably not go down too well with her, given the already good start.

Isaac thought to himself, "I'll get to my bedroom and unpack and perhaps pop over to the pub for an hour or two to meet some of the locals," but it wasn't to be. His room was quite spacious, with a bed so soft that you disappear into it. Everything else in the room looked like it had come straight off the set of a period drama. He half suspected a Victorian chambermaid of knocking on the door and asking to turn the bed down. As he lay there, he thought, "I don't really want to do anything, except go to sleep. I just don't have the energy," and by now he was beginning to enjoy sleep. Ironically, from past many years, he had lived by the saying, "we'll get plenty of sleep when we're dead."

He must have gone out completely cold because when he opened his eyes again, the light was seeping through the curtains and he could hear the birds singing. In fact, there seemed to be a bit of commotion outside. Isaac got out of the bed, still fully clothed from the night before and opened the curtains. To his surprise, there were many people milling about, sheep, cows, chickens. Stalls were being erected in the main square of the village as if it was a Saturday market. Though, he couldn't say for certain as he had never visited such a market before and had only seen them on the TV. The funny part was, it was only 6.30 in the morning. "What is wrong with these people?" he thought. "Don't they have homes that they can stay in?" Isaac washed in his little sink at the corner of the room, shaved, and got dressed again. He made his way down for breakfast. The time was 7 am, so he proceeded to find the dining room. In the light of day, the house was much bigger than he had first perceived. Though it looked small from the outside, the interiors seemed to be extensively spread. So after checking many rooms, he finally found a sign on one of the doors - 'Breakfast Room.' The room housed about seven random tables and chairs. He just picked one of them and sat. He noticed a series of boxes and bowls on the sideboard, but there were no croissants, fruit, or cold meat. What were you supposed to eat? Just then, Mrs. McDougal appeared as if from nowhere.

"You can't sit there; that is for Mr. and Mrs. Stanley from Worcestershire, and they sit there every day."

"Well," Isaac replied, "Where shall I sit?"

"Anywhere else," she answered, "but there! As I said."

"Yes, I've got it. Mr. and Mrs. Stanley from Worcestershire have to sit here!" Isaac shuffled over to the nearest table.

"Right, what would you like for breakfast? A full Scottish, or something else. Toast and marmalade or something else on toast?"

"No, I think I'll have a full Scottish, what does that entail?"

"Bacon, eggs, sausage, beans, black pudding and toast," Mrs. McDougal barked.

"Oh, just like an English Breakfast then?"

"NO! It is a full SCOTTISH breakfast!"

"Yes, I know that, but…Oh never mind, one of those please." Isaac was getting confused and didn't think he would win an argument with Mrs. McDougal.

"And would you like tea or coffee?"

Isaac asked, "Have you got any fresh orange?"

"Did I say fresh orange?"

"No…just coffee then. Thank you."

Isaac could feel the urge welling inside to tear a strip off her for her rude manner, but by then he was getting too hungry to bother and did not want to delay breakfast further. Within a short time, his full Scottish breakfast arrived. It was dripping with grease, piled on the plate like yesterday's waste and it tasted absolutely fantastic! Isaac must have been hungry. He had missed dinner and supper the day before as all he had wanted to do was drive and had become overwhelmed with the scenery around him. He could not have eaten, as there was just too much to see. Isaac sat back after devouring his breakfast, four rounds of toast and two coffees, wondering whether he could stand as he was so full.

Mrs. McDougal suddenly appeared again. "Are you finished, Mr. Montgomery?"

"Yes, thank you, and compliments to the chef," he said a little sarcastically.

"Oh," she replied, almost as if to insinuate they may have sabotaged the breakfast in some way.

"What will you be doing with yourself today?" Mrs. McDougal asked. Isaac had to ask her to repeat the question as her accent was too broad, he could not catch it all. Thankfully she didn't seem to mind.

"Well," he replied, "I thought I would find the local tourist information and perhaps have a good look around."

"Well, you will find a street map on the shelf by the door, and there is another map of the surrounding areas - whatever you like, walking, fishing or just sightseeing. I am afraid there is no golf course around here…it's much too hilly for that."

"Thanks very much for your help. I did wonder where to start, as my car isn't going anywhere; it is completely blocked by the market people."

Mrs. McDougal asked, "Do you know how long you will be staying?"

"I'm not quite sure. Could we take it one week at a time, and if things change I will give you plenty of notice?"

"Yes, that should be fine; we're not that busy this time of the year. Well, you have a good day Mr. Montgomery and I will see you later."

"As you can see, you have two keys. One is for the front door, so let yourself in, whatever time of day it is. I'll just ask you to be quiet if it's late. We don't want to disturb the other guests."

So, Isaac wore his coat and went out. It was extremely cold; good weather for the polar bears. As it turned out, Isaac was way overdressed in his Armani suit, three-quarter length Cromby, and his Italian brogues, complimented by a stunning Rolex on his arm. While all around him was a compliment of Wax jackets, Wellington boots, overalls, a variety of big woolen jumpers, padded shirts, wooly hats and high visibility jackets – and that was just the woman. He decided that he would have to find a local clothes shop and dress down a bit if he wanted to fit in. There were a variety of shops, but by the look of it, most were closed for the winter. There were no proper restaurants; just a little café, a fish and chips shop, and two pubs, The Dead Man's Chest and The Dipping Tank. There was also a huge hotel and a series of small B&Bs. As he moved further, he saw a small garage with two pumps, one ramp and an assortment of bric-a-brac they sold. One shop that Isaac did find open was a charity shop, so Isaac entered there wondering if they would have anything in his size. It was quite a large shop with an array of things. He could overhear the ladies talking. "He must be one of those city slickers by the way he is dressed. Looking for heirlooms and antiques, no doubt. If he wants to buy anything, we will charge him double."

"Right you are, Mrs. McCluff," said Mary.

They watched Isaac closely as he walked around, quite confused at the fact that he was looking for clothes. That didn't make sense to the ladies. Isaac was just out of earshot by then, but he could imagine what the conversation would be.

"He's up to no good…I tell you, Mary. Why does he want old clothes? That doesn't make sense?"

As Isaac looked further he came across a jacket, the type that fishermen wear, along with a couple of pairs of jeans, some shirts that looked as if they had come out of an old Western, and a discarded pair of boots that could quite possibly have belonged to Frankenstein. Isaac thought, "That will do for now until I can find a proper clothes shop." So he paid his bill of £12, which was double. He thought back and wondered that he would have paid more for a cup of cappuccino in Chelsea. He left the shop and began to walk again when he came across a supermarket, 'Millicent Stewart's Groceries and Post Office.'

Isaac thought to himself, "This really is a new experience. I have never actually been shopping. Normally, I would order what I need online and nine out of ten times, I dined out." He couldn't get over the fact that how small these buildings looked from outside, but once you went in – after hitting the door with your face, as these were not automatic – they just seemed to stretch. The best part was everything was super cheap. Also, they had a cash machine for withdrawals.

Just then, a low and charming voice asked, "Can I help you with anything sir?"

"I must admit," said Isaac, "I am looking for clothes, but I might be in the wrong shop?"

"Oh no sir, don't worry, they're right at the back of the store, and if you require any help, please feel free to seek me."

She was a woman aged about 45 to 50, with an English accent, an enchanting smile, and the voice of an angel. In her day, Isaac imagined, she would have broken some hearts. Even now her demeanour was that of a sophisticated woman and she was so impeccably dressed. She just didn't seem to be the kind of woman that would run a grocery store. Perhaps, like Isaac, she was someone trying to escape her past. This intrigued Isaac. As time went on, he was curious to find out her story and perhaps what she had run away from.

With that, Isaac snapped back to the task at hand - finding clothing. He bought some more shirts, some newer looking jeans, a scarf, a wooly hat and a pair of what they called 'Dealers boots'. However, he would not compromise on his underwear. They had to be used for protection from the clothes he had just bought. It was now late morning, so he decided to go back to his room and get changed, before exploring the local market and probably going to the pub for some lunch. Isaac changed from his dapper, man about town appearance into a cross between a cowboy and a fisherman's friend. He then proceeded with his voyage of discovery.... to the market.

It was like a different world. He couldn't believe his eyes, as he strolled aimlessly around the stalls and animal pens. He had walked out of the real world straight onto the set of Mad Max with animals everywhere - cows, chickens, sheep, and dogs. A variety of characters hustling around. Isaac had to admit that he was overwhelmed by it all. However, he just found himself drawn in even further. He wanted to see everything there was to see. They had fish stalls, beef burger stalls, and the food was awesome. If he wasn't from a different side of life, he could think of nothing better. He could barely even understand half of the conversations that were going on in the marketplace. The market was totally surrounded by a ring of 4X4s and an assortment of vans and trucks, it was like the event was being staged…right in the middle of a scrap yard. For the first time in his life, he felt a state of exhilaration in his life other than when chasing money on the stock market. That was all he had known for so long, along with the restaurants and nightclubs. Now, he was totally away from it all and he was enjoying himself without the complication and concerns for the company that had swallowed him entirely. He was almost like a child seeing things for the first time. With a fresh perspective on the world around him, he was slowly learning the lessons that had to be learned to evolve in his growth and understanding and to become the person he would eventually like to be. He understood nothing but the city, and right now that could have been another planet somewhere in the Solar System!

"Right," Isaac thought, "off to the pub. I'll go to the Dipping Tank; it's just opposite the B&B and I won't have to go far to my bed."

The pub was absolutely rammed with people. There was standing room only, even though it was a big pub. Isaac didn't mind, as it was like a Saturday night out at home with everybody trying to get into the nightclubs. There was perhaps just one difference - the fragrance of Chanel and Gucci had transformed to the smell of cow dung, sweat musk and other smells that Isaac didn't want to think about. There were sounds of people singing from the corner; Isaac thought that they were local folk songs. Then pub had a hard type of flooring, but it was very sticky to walk on. Sawdust had been sprinkled everywhere, probably to soak up the spills and other fluids. Isaac felt totally out of his depth, but he pushed onto the bar.

A gruff voice asked, "What do you want?"

"A pint of lager, please."

The man shouted to one of the women behind the bar, "A pint of lager for Mr. Namby-Pamby."

Isaac thought to himself, "I must remember not to say 'please', I think it is a forgotten concept here." Isaac received his drink, and so did most of his sleeve. He made a strategic withdrawal to an empty corner, where he could stand back and watch the festivities play out. Everybody seemed to be talking at the top of their voices, every second word being a profanity and a string of colourful metaphors, mainly from big men with hard faces, with skin like leather, anvils where hands used to be and cuts and bruises from living such a hard life. They were nudging and bumping into each other. Occasionally, two men would stop and square up to each other with evil intent, as if at any moment they would erupt into anger. Then there would be a nod and everybody would carry on as if nothing had happened. There were dogs everywhere, barking and yelping. A quick kick and they would lie down, then another would start. Then, as if by magic, the pub cleared out. The auctions must have started. Isaac utilised the opportunity and hurriedly got back to the bar to order his second pint and grab a bar stool right in the corner. He really didn't want to get in their way, when they all come back. In London, every morning Isaac would work out at the gym before work. He was about 16 stone of muscle and a good amateur boxer, but the sort of people he had just seen looked like they would pick him up and spit him out like a well-chewed piece of tobacco while holding a pint in the other hand. At this Isaac decided to try to blend into the background. He was glad that he had changed his clothes. If he had walked in earlier in what he was wearing, he would have been hung, drawn and quartered and sold for meat on the market.

Just then the door flew open. "Oh no!" he thought "They are coming back. That was a quick auction." But to his delight, it was all womenfolk. They must have bought what they needed and it was their turn for a little tipple, while the men engaged in the wheeling and dealing. Isaac had to admit it was so much quieter than before. Though, as it started to fill, he started feeling like a bit of a lemon sitting on the corner of the bar. The door opened once more. Isaac couldn't believe the apparition that stood before him, as he remembered the words Phil had told him, "That's the woman I am going to marry one day." She had long, wavy auburn hair, totally unkempt, wild and free; the complexion of a porcelain doll; a smile that lit up the room, and eyes bluer than the blue of the crystal waters of a mountain stream. She quietly asked a lady next to her if she would like a drink from the bar. Isaac assumed she was her mother.

"No, thank you, Beth. I have just got one." It was like Isaac had been in a dark place for a long time, where a door just opened and a light flooded in. Isaac could never remember feeling so mesmerised by a woman. She wore a long wool jumper with an ill-fitted shirt and what looked like a pair of Jackboots. She seemed to have no real shape to her, as her clothes all seemed far too big for her frame. As she walked to the bar, it was a wonder that Isaac's eyes didn't burn straight through her. Contrarily, she just glanced at Isaac and almost looked straight through him. It seemed definitely one sided. Isaac had fallen headlong in love with the woman. He thought, "This must be my punishment for being a complete and utter bastard to women in the life beforehand." He decided he just had to get out of there because by now knew that he was a jumble of words and shaking as if he couldn't breathe. He just couldn't stay there any longer. What was happening could be compared to the butterflies of aspiration that something exciting was going to happen. But for now, she didn't even realise that he existed and he would have to leave it at that. Isaac collected himself and walked towards the door. He caught Beth from the corner of his eye and she smiled. Isaac smiled back, but his heart was trying to jump out of his chest. He took a deep breath; his mind was racing, his thoughts were all over the place. He kept thinking, "This should not be happening. I have never felt like this before. There is no way you can see somebody and feel the way I do. I know nothing about her - she could be married, with children, and content with her life. If this is love, then I don't think I really like it! Going from a level headed calculated personality to a blithering idiot in minutes, with no control of my thoughts or words. I just need to get back to my room and think this out."

Again he was going through a bit of a quandary. Feelings like this hadn't existed in his life before. He hadn't come here to find romance, he just wanted to get away from his problems. But to think it from another perspective, his feelings towards others was a part of that problem. Pondering deep into the night, he asked himself ridiculous questions, picturing different scenarios of his life with this woman beside him - "would I live in London or stay in Corngurn? Would she want me? How could I get to speak to her? Should I just pack up and go home? Why am I putting myself through this?" There seemed to be no logic at all. Amidst all these musings, he slowly drifted off to sleep.

CHAPTER FOUR

Love in Corngurn

Isaac woke up the following morning. It was about 10am and the first thought that came to his mind was the woman that he saw in the bar that night - Beth. He wanted to find out more about her...but how? He had already missed the breakfast. So, he got dressed in his new shabby attire and went on to hunt for some food. Luckily, the café was open. He had a full Scottish breakfast. All through, he was peering out of the window, hoping for a sight of Beth. However, he knew that even if he had seen her, he wouldn't have had a clue as to what to say. He really needed to know more about her, and that would take time. So, for now, he wasn't going anywhere, until one way or the other, he found out something about her. As he peered out of the window, he noticed how quiet everything was compared to the previous day. It was almost like a ghost town with very few people mulling about. He thought that it would certainly be a good day to walk around and find out more about the village, its history and the people that lived there. First, he went down to the harbour. There were lots of fishing boats, small cruisers, and other titbits that you associate with a harbour. There was a fish auction room, all bordered by holiday homes and retirement apartments. It looked like most of the harbour could have been built in the 18th century. The weather had definitely taken its toll on the fortress type walls, which were now badly eroded and missing in places. But it didn't seem to matter, it just added to the overall look and the old world charm. There still old fisherman, who were repairing their nets and painting their boats in order to be ready for whatever the winter would bring. They had badly rolled cigarettes hanging from the sides of their mouths, some of them looked like old bone pipes chuffing out foul smelling odour. Their faces were cracked with well-worn skin, bushy eyebrows, unkempt beards, and teeth as yellow as the sun – that is, if they had teeth at all. This was years of legacy that passed from the father to son and taught how to make their livelihoods from the unforgiving sea. The cold sea did not spare anyone - from boys to men; it was the place of lost souls that the sea captured in the last 100 years. This made Isaac wonder, how we complain about our jobs in warm offices with the healthy and safe environment; about our cars with every conceivable extra; and our centrally heated houses. If even for a day, one has to go on one of these fishing boats, he would probably be dead before he got back to the harbour. One really needs to recognise how lucky he is by the grace of God. At the moment, the sun was shining and the sea was glistening; inviting for a swim. It just looked like a picture postcard. With adventure fading away on the horizon, Isaac followed the well-trodden pathway back towards the village. The houses around him reminded him of the sailors that were lost at sea and the families that remembered them. Their lives were lost while they were trying to feed their families and keep a roof over their heads. It was an extremely humbling experience, as Isaac read the plaques of remembrance. Once back in the village square, Isaac decided to sit on a bench opposite a large statue in the middle of the village. The statue was of a boy holding a lantern on the end of a long road. The plaque went on to describe that in 1922 during a particularly bad winter, the boy had stood at the end of the harbour wall guiding the fishing boats in from the stormy sea, bringing them back to safety. Nobody ever knew his name or who he was, and after that night he was never seen again. But whenever there is a particularly bad storm, one can see a light glowing in the distance, and it is alight till the last boat safely reaches the harbour.

The village, Isaac noticed, seemed to have a uniformity about it. The houses were all made of the same brick or rock, almost as if the entire village had been built at the same time. But it was not so; it was actually constructed over the years, which was evident from the highs and the lows of the buildings. These buildings stretched from the harbour onto the hill; all commanded a view of the harbour and the sea. You could tell by the rock discolouration that the houses had been built at different times. There were also some shops intermingled with private houses. Pubs, although only two, set quite a commanding presence within the community and there was a church that overlooked everything. There were narrow winding roads snaking their way from top to bottom with the sun shining down upon them. It looked so beautiful, but in the depths of winter, it must have been treacherous. Thankfully, for a while, all this had distracted Isaac's mind, but again the thoughts of Beth started troubling him. "Where can I start?" Isaac thought. "I know…I will go to that supermarket and see that lovely woman, Millicent. I will try and engage her in a conversation and see if there is any way that she can help me in this quest to find this mystery woman."

***

As Isaac walked into the supermarket on the pretense of buying a *Financial Times* and basically just to look around, he once again heard that charming voice, "Can I help you, sir?"

"Oh no, thanks. I'm just after a paper and something to eat."

"Are you staying long in Corngurn?" she asked.

"I'm not quite sure, just taking it one day at a time for now," replied Isaac, "…but it really is an engaging place!"

Millicent replied, "Yes, I like it here. My husband and I have been living here for about 10 years now and for the most part, the people are quite nice."

Isaac replied, "I hope you don't think I am being nosey, but I was having a drink at the pub the other day and there was a young woman that came in. I think her name was Beth. She looked in her mid to late 20s with long wavy, auburn hair. She was wearing a big wooly jumper and Jackboots…that's what I think you call them? I must admit I was quite taken with her. I didn't speak to her, in case she was married or seeing someone. So, I decided to find out a little bit more about her, before I make a fool of myself."

"Well," Millicent replied, "I think I know the young lady in question. That will be Beth McCoogan. She lives just a short distance from the village, on the McCoogan's farm with her family. They're tenant farmers on Lord Stewart's estate. They are quite a big family of four brothers and four sisters. Their mother is a lovely woman called Morag but the father is not an easy man to deal with, Big Mac McCoogan.

She paused, gave a big smile and continued, "So, the answer to your question is yes. Yes, of course, I know Beth. She really is a natural beauty like you say, but I should tell you that eight years ago she was married to one of the local boys here. I think his name was David McLaughlin. They had a son called Mac. He was about 5 years old when David and little Mac went fishing one day, just beyond the harbour walls and went missing. They were found about a week later, washed up on Smuggler's Cove. Nobody knows what happened on that day, but the result was unchangeable. They both had drowned and Beth had lost her husband and her son, all in one day. On the day of the funeral, the whole village had turned out and people from far and wide came to show their respects. Since that day, Beth has vowed that she would never love again. In fact, for two years she lived as a recluse in the house, where she, David and little Mac had lived happily. Eventually, her parents and family got her to move back into her maternal home to help her start living a life again. For a long time, she was almost willing herself to death as had become very ill and frail. It was a long road back for her. Though this happened a few years ago, you can still see her every now and then, walking near the harbour wall, looking at the sea, as if she would once again see David and little Mac fishing happily. So, although I would love to see her happy again and so would so many others, I don't think anybody would ever be able to break the spell that she is under. She loved once, and for some once is more than enough. I am really sorry young man, you might be on a fool's errand if you think you could have a relationship with Beth."

Isaac was stunned and at the same time, he felt immense grief for Beth. He said, "Thanks a lot Millicent for telling me about her. It really is a tragic story; to have loved intensely and then have it taken away traumatically. I can imagine that she would have preferred dying with her, instead of living without them. It humbled me earlier when I was reading some of the plaques around the harbour. It was unsettling to see that so many people have lost their lives at sea and many loved ones had to carry on with their lives with this pain over the years. One thing I must say about Beth is that she is an intensely strong woman to have brought herself back from that dark period. Although, I am sure that a lot of people must have helped her, but if she didn't have the strength herself, nobody could have saved her."

"Yes, I suppose you're right. She is a strong woman."

"Oh well, I came here to get away from the city and to try and find myself. I wanted to decide what I want to do with the rest of my life," said Isaac.

"Well, for the most part, this is a very quiet place; you should be able to think, if nothing else."

"Yes, that's the hope."

"Just the paper then?"

"Yes please, and thank you for the chat."

"It is quiet this time of year, so it is nice to have someone to talk to. If you don't mind me asking, what did you do before you came here?"

"I was a banker in London."

"That answers my question," said Millicent, "as when you came here the first time, your clothes were impeccable. Your shoes, your manicured nails, your Rolex watch…you were just so out of place."

"Yes, that is why I bought these clothes and boots. I stood out like a money lender. I would probably be beaten to death by nightfall, and that would have wrecked my plans of finding what it is I am looking for."

"Well, that's true! Millicent said with a smile. "Have a nice day sir."

"Please, call me Isaac."

"Well, I'm Millicent…nice to meet you, Isaac. I hope you find what you are looking for."

"Thank you; have a good day." He smiled.

After coming out from the supermarket, Isaac decided to go to the pub. As he walked his mind just kept wandering back to Beth and the life she had lived. He thought, "It seems so unfair. She had everything she must have wanted, but it was all snatched away. Life can be such a cruel mistress. We never know what it has in store for us the next second. That is why I think we must reach out and take what we want while we can. We should never put off something that we can do today for tomorrow." And for the first time in Isaac's life, this thought was not regarding making more money. Isaac had decided that he would stay for as long as it took and would try to get to know Beth McCoogan. Something in him had told him that there was a reason why he was there. From the instant he saw her, he had felt something that he had never felt before. So for him, this was the sign. Perhaps he could try to bring her back to life once more and in the process find true love. But this, only time would tell.

CHAPTER FIVE

Serendipity

AFTER THAT DAY, THE TIME just seemed to fly by. Three months had gone and Isaac was still in the village. By now, he had rented a small cottage. It was the last one on the right; this was how he addressed the house and how everybody else knew it. He saw Beth quite often in the shops and walking around the harbour, but could never seem to find an opportune moment to speak to her. If she ever saw Isaac, she would always give him a big smile. But they never talked. She would just walk on like she was in a world of her own, alone with her thoughts. Isaac longed to talk to her; he used to run through in his mind a million times, what he plans to say to her. But the truth was he didn't have a clue. She was still in pain, and he thought, that regardless of what he says, his words would seem empty to her. Isaac spent many nights on call with Phil back in London. Phil was a logical man. He would simply say, "You've got no chance, you should move on. You have never been short of female company."

"You know Phil, you can be a complete and utter arse when you want to. Put Pen on the call, if she will talk to me," Isaac responded.

"Hello Isaac, what's this idiot telling you to do now?"

Isaac had already filled them in about Beth's story and how he felt when he first saw her.

"What am I going to do Pen?" Isaac asked. "Am I wrong to pursue someone who seems so lost, and why do I feel I need to? Who do I think I am that I can wave a magic wand and everything will be ok?"

"Well, Isaac," Pen sighed, "this woman has been deeply hurt in her life. She needs time. I won't kid you, she may never even be ready to commit to another relationship, as her first one ended tragically. The only thing you can do is just be there, and if it's meant to be then it will happen all by itself. And if it doesn't, remember, we don't always get what we want, or I would be with George Clooney and not Philip!"

"I heard that!" Philip shouted.

"Shut up and watch your cartoons, you big baby," Pen scolded. "I must be marrying him for his money because it is definitely not for his mind. On a serious note Isaac, just be patient and if it is meant to be, it will be. Oh, and by the way, the gang asked how you are. I haven't told them where you are staying, but it might be nice if you could just call them and let them know that you are ok."

"I'm sorry, I must admit I haven't even turned my phone on since I got here. I just use this pay as you go to call you and Phil. Just tell them, I send my best, but I am not ready yet. I will send them all a Christmas card," Isaac explained.

"Oh, that's three months away. You really aren't coming back, are you?" Pen enquired.

"Well no, I am going to give this my best chance. Oh, and you'll never guess; I've got a part-time job at the pub. Also, I might have a bit of work on one of the farms around here too. Shearing sheep of all things. That's if I can turn my hand to it. People are always looking for cheap labour around here."

"You have got to be kidding me! The great Isaac Montgomery, the golden child of the stock market, shearing sheep. You are absolutely minted; you never need to work again."

"No," Isaac replied, "but I really am enjoying these new challenges. I am even thinking about painting."

"What, people's houses?" Pen gasped.

"No, painting pictures silly. I'm really on a high and I want to do everything."

"Well I think you are nuts, but if it makes you happy, that's great."

"Anyway, thanks for the talk Pen. Say goodbye to Philip for me and I'll speak to you soon."

After keeping down the phone, Isaac sat and thought about the conversation. "Pen was right about Beth. She may never be ready to seek love again, but I will be there in case the occasion arises, and that means keeping busy, with a variety of jobs. I feel that I am set for the challenge." As Isaac sat there deep in thought, he remarked, "Well another day over and I can't wait for the morning." Isaac seemed to be sleeping well lately. It was like a fog had been lifted.

***

The following day, it was his training at the Dipping Tank pub. At the crack of dawn, Isaac had some breakfast and went on his way to the pub.

Isaac never thought that he would say that you can find him in a pub at 9 am on the dot. The landlord, Mr. O'Leary, opened the door and let him in. He explained the tills, showed Isaac where the mop and bucket were, and taught him how to pull a pint, although to begin with they were just pints of froth. Anyway, he got the hang of it after a short while. As far as the money was concerned, he could do it in seconds without a till. It would be a great chance for him to meet a lot more locals. Three nights a week and variable weekends, and £6.20 an hour. Isaac thought how, back in London, he could make £2 million in 30 minutes on the stock exchange, but he was really pleased with this £6.20 an hour. Isaac thought, "I have gone nuts, and I feel so much better for it."

"Right," said Mr. O'Leary, "you have got three nights this week, Tuesday, Thursday and Friday, and Saturday is the market day so we are extra busy from 10 in the morning until midnight. Are you ok with that?"

"Yes, that's fine," Isaac replied. He was really looking forward to it.

Mr. O'Leary said, "On Saturday I'll be about, but you will mainly be working with our head barmaid, Summer. If you have any problems, just ask her and she will put you right. If you don't mind me asking, where do you come from?"

Isaac replied, "Well, I have lived in London most of my life."

Mr. O'Leary enquired, "So, what brings you to Corngurn? It is very far and a lot different from the big city? Couldn't you cut it there? Your mannerisms and the way you speak, don't go together with the clothes you are wearing. I get the impression you would feel more comfortable in a suit, and you are obviously well educated. You are like a fish out of water here. I have worked all over England, on the motorways and cities. I saved until I had enough money to buy my own pub. One fine day, fifteen years ago, I came here to build a road. We decided to stay in Corngurn, this pub came up for sale and the rest is history, but you, what is your story?"

"Well, you are right, of course, I worked in a bank as a cashier. Day in and day out, I just didn't seem to have any challenge. One day, I was googling a holiday destination on my computer and somewhere along the way Corngurn Village came up with the results. So I read all about it and I thought, 'I have got some holidays left, I would like to visit this place.' When I came here, I loved the place so much, that I haven't gone back. But, of course, my savings are running out now, hence I started looking for a job."

"You wait until winter comes…you will wish you had gone back home. Anyway, welcome aboard. Your first shift starts tomorrow and we will see you then," Mr. O'Leary instructed.

So, 6 pm the following day Isaac worked for the first of his three nights and he met a variety of characters. They named him "poofter boy" due to the way that he spoke and because his clothes were far too smart for the bar. However they had accepted him – the bunch of 'red necks,' Isaac thought. After the first few shifts under his belt, it was Saturday and he remembered from his early days the first time he had gone into the pub on a market day. As he entered, it was wall to wall with people, so this would be his baptism of fire. 10 am on the dot he walked in to find a lovely young lady behind the bar. "You must be Summer," he asked. "The head barmaid?"

"Yes, and you are Isaac? The boss said that I should expect you. Right, you haven't worked a Saturday before?"

"No," Isaac replied.

"Well, between about 11 and 12, before the auctions start, it gets very busy. The clients will come at you from everywhere. You just have to try and keep an eye on who is next and just keep serving. You may find that you are being called a multitude of names and the language will probably shock you. But, then that's the way it is hereabouts. If you face any problem, just give me a shout and I will throw the bastards out!" She was such a pretty little thing, about 5 feet tall, 8-9 stone wringing wet, but Isaac believed her when she said it. A feisty little minx. The day rolled on with a few minor arguments. Isaac learned many new words, eloquently put like, "Fuck face get me a dram," and, "Are you a bleeding poof?" or, "I'm talking to you, you sheep's arse," but Isaac had to admit that all this made him smile.

It was nearly 7 when the rush started reducing and it wasn't quite so busy. Watching Summer with these people was like watching a shepherd with her crook. She handled them beautifully, and Isaac couldn't recall anyone having an argument with her or even a stern word. Isaac thought to himself, "Well, if she did have a problem, no doubt she must have sent them to see me….the new boy, but luckily, I just let it go over my head."

"Well Summer, we didn't do too badly and every time it got very busy, Mr. O'Leary came and helped."

Summer replied, "He did this week, but next Saturday we will be on our own."

"I take it you live locally, Summer?" Isaac asked.

"Yes, I live with my parents and family about a mile out of town, McCoogan Farm. I have four brothers and three sisters, two sisters-in-law and a brother-in-law. We have lived here all our lives and generations before us."

Isaac was ecstatic. Eagerly, he asked, "I hope you don't mind me asking, you have a sister called Beth, right?"

"Yes, why do you ask?"

"I think when I first came in here, I remember her with who I assumed was your mother. She looked very sad."

"Well she has faced a lot of tragedy in her life and you don't need to know about it. She likes to keep to herself and that's all I will say on the subject."

Isaac quickly responded, "I'm sorry, I must have touched a nerve. I didn't mean to be nosey."

"No I'm sorry, there are just some things that are better left unsaid. I love my sister dearly, but do wish she could move forward with her life. I think her thoughts are very much stuck in the past."

Just then the door opened, and two men and Beth walked in. One of the men said, "Any chance of a freebie sis?"

"Hello Beth," said Summer. "I know I told you to come and have a drink with me, but did you have to bring Jimmy and Wallace to lower the tone of the place?"

"Ah go on, give us a freebie sis," repeated Jimmy

"Ah piss off, you'll pay like everybody else Jimmy!"

"Isaac!" Summer shouted. "Come and meet two of my half-wit brothers and my sister, Beth."

"How do you do? I'm Isaac," he said nervously.

"Oh," Wallace replied, "so you're the Nancy boy we've heard about? Well, you are very pretty, I will give you that."

"Leave him alone, Wallace and drink your drink, you sheep shagger," Summer came to the rescue.

"Who told you that?

"Jimmy."

"And this is my sister, Beth." Summer introduced her to Isaac.

"Hello, it is really nice to meet you, at last. I've seen you around the village and you always have a big smile, or you rare too polite to laugh?"

Isaac heard the voice he had been wanting to hear for so long, "Oh, it's nice to meet you too, Isaac. I did wonder who you were and why you were in Corngurn."

Isaac explained, "I just wanted to get away from London to a quieter way of life, and I fell in love with you....umm...sorry, I mean your village. I don't know where my head is at the moment. Sorry again!"

"That's ok. I'm forever getting my words mixed up." Beth smiled.

"I know this might sound a bit forward, but if you ever have time, I would love if you could show me some of those really lovely pathways through the hills. They are said to be breathtakingly beautiful with the views of the sea and the cliff tops." Isaac inquired.

"No, I'm sorry...I am always busy during the day on the farm."

"I hope I haven't offended you by asking that? That's the last thing I want to do!"

"Oh no, it's just that we are very busy at the moment and I am needed on the farm."

"Do you want to play a game of darts, Jimmy?" Wallace said, trying to change the conversation.

"No, I am sick of beating you!" Jimmy replied. "Beth, will you do the dart board, please? You know I'm bad with sums."

"Ok, I will do that, but then I want to go home."

"Isaac, you have customers," Summer called Isaac.

"Sorry, Summer I will get straight to it." Isaac hurriedly served the two men at the end of the bar.

"Isaac?"

"Yes, Summer?"

"What was all that about with Beth?"

"I just asked her if she would show me some of the walks around here."

"Right. I am going to ask this only once - do you fancy my sister?"

"Yes, I do."

"Ok, tell me about your life. Have you been married before and are you running away from it? Do you have children? Why have you really come to Corngurn?"

"I have never been married. I have no children. I was sick of my life in London and so I decided to call it quits. I accidentally came across this place on Google and thought it was a lovely place to escape to. I had some savings which are now running out, so I am now trying to pay my own way, so I can stay. I love being a part of this village," Isaac explained.

"So what you're telling me is you are a 30-year-old man, who has had a crisis in his life and has run away from it with not a pot to piss in? Just the clothes on your back and you want to go out with my sister? Even if I could help you, I won't!"

Isaac quickly came back with, "Oh, but I have a trust fund of £50,000 that I would get when I turn 30, and that's next week. How do you feel about that, young wench?"

"How do you feel about younger women? Say around 25?" Summer asked mischievously.

"Well I think they are fantastic, but I have set my sights on somebody older!" Isaac replied

"You bastard!" Summer said with a cheeky smile. "You have been here for three or four months now. Nothing stays quiet in this village, so knowing the gossip around here, you must have heard Beth's story if you have been asking about her?"

"Yes, I had heard and it is such a sorry tale."

"WHO TOLD YOU?"

"To be honest, I would prefer not to tell that. So let's just say I have heard about her husband and son drowning sadly."

"Knowing all that, why do you want to go out with her?"

"Well before I knew anything about her life, she walked into the pub that fateful day and she took my breath away. I don't think she even noticed me, but for me, it was like I had been searching for her all my life and I didn't even know that."

"Christ, you sure you're not gay?"

Isaac replied with a giggle, "No, that would be too much of a pain in the arse. So will you help me, Summer?"

"As for her not noticing you, I remember her saying that she had seen a handsome stranger in the pub that she hadn't seen before. Did you see him?"

"Yeah right, good one," Isaac joked.

"Well I will try to help you, but I can't promise anything. What we all want for her is that she starts living her life again. It has been a few years now and she has been almost a recluse all that time. But, she has started to get out a little more lately and has started joining in with things. Anyway, you have customers….it is getting busy again," Summer said, looking around, "That's why we stay open until 12 on a Saturday."

"Right, Herr Kommandant, back to work it is."

"And less of that, batty boy," Summer laughed.

Isaac thought, "My new nickname." With that, he started serving once more. All of the time his eyes were drawn back to the chalkboard, where Beth was standing. Whenever he caught her eye, she would just smile. His heart would swell and he could feel it beating vigorously in his chest.

So the night rolled on and she wasn't leaving the dynamic duo. They were still playing darts and she seemed quite happy to stay. Isaac remarked to Summer, "I thought Beth wanted to go home early?"

"Yes, so did I, but they are probably waiting to walk me home after my shift."

"Will they walk me home?" asked Isaac. "It's very dark outside."

"Get on with you, Nancy boy," laughed Summer.

"Will one of these names eventually stick, because I don't know which to answer to? I'm getting confused. I must admit, though, it has been a pleasure working with you. You have a fantastic sense of humour."

Isaac hoped that she was sincere when she promised to help him connect to Beth a little better. About 11.30 pm, it began to slow down and people started to leave. Wallace and Jimmy were, by this stage, a little drunk. They must have sunk about 15 pints each. It was hard enough to understand them when they were sober, so now that they were drunk, Isaac had no chance.

Summer said, "We're closing the bar down now, so if they ask you for another drink, tell them to see me because they will probably threaten you if you say no. They are certainly drunk enough."

"You know, I can handle myself."

"Yes I know, but how is wanking going to help?" Summer jested.

"You have a filthy mind!" exclaimed Isaac.

"Yes I am aware; it is one of my best features. I'll just pop out the back and have a cig," said Summer. "Then we'll shut down the bar in five minutes.

"Oh great, leave me with Tweedle Dumb and Tweedle Dumber," Isaac sarcastically replied.

"Hey, they are my brothers you are talking about, and if I could think of any better way to describe them, I would give you an argument. Back in 5." With that, Summer quickly disappeared.

"Hello Beth, I didn't see you there. Can I help you?"

"Could I have two more pints for my brothers?" Summer requested.

"I am sorry, I am under strict instructions not to serve them any more beer, and if they want one they will have to talk to Summer."

Beth looked at Isaac with a sad smile. "I must apologise for their behaviour and the names they have called you tonight."

"No, that's no problem, all in the nature of the job," Isaac said with a kind look. "Summer will be back in a minute. She has just gone for a cig, and as I said earlier, I am very pleased to have met you properly at last, and again I hope I didn't offend you earlier, asking about the walks around here."

All of a sudden Summer was back.

"Cash up the tills and let's get out of here."

"Right, that's me back to work," Isaac explained. "See you later Beth, I better go before your sister docks my pay." Within ten minutes, the cashing up was done, and as Summer said, they were out of there.

Summer turned to Isaac. "It was nice to work with you, Isaac."

"Thank you, Summer," Isaac replied. "Goodnight everybody!" Isaac shouted as they began to leave the premises.

Just then Isaac heard someone call his name. "Isaac! Beth wants to talk to you." Isaac turned and walked towards the bar, trying to contain his excitement.

When he approached, Beth was glowing as she asked, "Isaac, I will try to get some time off to take you on some of the walks around here, if you are still interested?"

"Oh that would be fantastic; I will look forward to that."

Isaac was ecstatic. Of all of the ways he had imagined speaking to her, all of a sudden out of the blue she was there, right in front of him. He was flying as high as a kite, with no drugs involved. It was like all of his dreams had come true, even though he didn't have a date yet. He thought, "At last, I have a chance and that is all I wanted. Now I am happy to go back to my cold damp house, the last house on the right." Isaac honestly thought if he had wanted he could have flown there, he was feeling so high on life. He was experiencing so many feelings that he had never felt before. For the first time, he could imagine a future with somebody else in his life. Isaac decided that he would wait as long as it took. He cannot afford to blow this chance. He pondered on the fact that he had told Summer a lie about his trust fund and his job in London. Isaac just wanted to be seen as an ordinary bloke, not some multi-millionaire, who was born with a silver spoon in his mouth. "I want Beth to love me the same way I love her. The only basis of that love should be that we want to be together with each other. And if for some reason, it is not to be, then I will respect her decision and move on with my broken heart dragging behind me." With these thoughts in mind, Isaac decided to call it for the day and headed home.

CHAPTER SIX

A new companion

As Isaac reached home, fumbling with his keys, he heard a crying sound from the nearby bush in front of the house. It was a little brown and white dog. It looked cold and wet and possibly hungry. Just as Isaac opened the door, the dog ran straight inside the house and lay in front of the fire. Isaac lit the gas and the little dog just lay there. Isaac thought, "He must have belonged to the last owners of the house." He decided to try and look at his tag, but the dog growled aggressively at him and bared his teeth.

"Ungrateful little shit!" Isaac muttered under his breath. Suddenly, he came up with an idea. "I have never had a pet, I can consider keeping it." He decided to make himself a cup of coffee and give the dog some of the leftovers from the day before. Isaac switched the fire down to one and went to bed thinking, "I will sort him out in the morning, so he may as well stay for the night." Lying in bed, Isaac began to ponder about the dog. "He might just be lost, his owners could be out looking for him right now…." Right at that moment, Isaac noticed the dog slipping into the bedroom and he jumped on the bed.

"If you want to stay here, your place is downstairs, Dog. This is my bedroom," Isaac commanded.

With that, the dog just lay down, turned his head and gave Isaac an evil stare. "Well," Isaac thought, "at this time of night, I cannot be arsed. Training will start tomorrow." Slowly, they both drifted off to sleep. Mind over mind, but for tonight the dog had won. Isaac was now his bitch.

The following day around 8 am, Isaac heard the sound of barking coming from downstairs. "Well, there goes my sleep-in plans," Isaac thought. "I better go and see what he wants." The dog was scratching at the kitchen door, so Isaac opened it and off the dog ran, like a stockbroker on speed. "Well, I'm up early. I will have a coffee, go to the shop, get a paper and see what is happening in the world. Probably the same old shit, just a different day." As soon as Isaac stepped out of the house, the dog was there again. He followed him all the way up to the shop. Once outside the shop, Isaac gestured at a spot. "Now you stay here." Isaac was amazed that he actually obeyed him and went to that spot to wait.

"Good morning Millicent, only me," Isaac said while entering the shop.

Millicent appeared from behind the counter. "Oh hello Isaac, nice to see you again. I see you have got a friend," she said, nodding at the doorway.

"Yes, I was going to ask you if you knew who the dog is or belongs to?" Isaac asked.

"Well he has been around for a month or two, but nobody knows where he is from' Millicent looked at the dog, smiled and added, "but it looks like he has adopted you now."

"I get that impression too. Well, I better get some dog food for him."

"How are things going with the new job?" Millicent enquired.

"I am getting the hang of it...it gives me a good chance to meet the locals. Also, I work with Summer McCoogan and she makes me laugh like crazy, but the best benefit is...I formally got introduced to her sister, Beth."

"Oh really? How is she? We don't see her out very often," Millicent asked, now looking very interested.

"Well, she seems well. She was out with Wallace and Jimmy."

"Oh, the terrible twins? If there is any trouble in the town, they will surely be the source. The only other possibility could be the McCredie's another family in the area."

"I have still got a lot to learn about this place. Have you got my *Financial Times*? I do like a good read on a Sunday."

"Yes, it is here under the counter. It seems a strange paper for a barman to be reading?" Millicent said mischievously.

"By the time you hear about the government's new plans and budgets, it is more comical than the *Sun*. My father always reads it, so even I have picked up the habit. I must admit I don't understand most of it, but if my father should call, it will give us something to talk about. Well, I better get going. Let's see if the dog follows me still." Isaac turned and almost banged into Mrs. McDougal. "Oh hello, Mrs. McDougal," he said as he almost knocked her flying.

"Hello, Mr. Montgomery."

"Sorry, I didn't see you standing there," Isaac apologised, before bidding goodbye. "See you tomorrow ladies."

"Bye Isaac," the women both echoed.

"Right dog, let's go home," Isaac said to the dog. Once they got home, Isaac immediately placed a frying pan on the cooktop. "I'll fix myself a nice big breakfast," he thought. He also opened a tin of dog food for his mysterious friend and placed it on the floor. As the dog came closer to smell the food, Isaac gently stroked him and got a glimpse of his tag. It said Jacamo. There was nothing else on the tag - no address or telephone number, just Jacamo. Anyway, he devoured the food and then went straight into the front room to sit near the fire once again. Isaac continued to prepare his breakfast and sat down to eat at the kitchen table.

Suddenly, there was a knock at the door. Isaac placed the dishes in the sink and went on to open the door. It was Summer.

"Didn't I see enough of you last night?" Isaac joked

"No, I was fully dressed, so hard luck."

"Well you better come in," Isaac said as he moved out of the doorway.

"Don't mind the dog; I think he has adopted me," Isaac explained. Just as he said that, Jacamo leaped at Summer for attention.

"Oh, he is a lovely Jack Russell, what's his name?"

"That's nice! He's all over you like a rash, but he won't come near me unless I'm feeding him or he is stealing my bed. His name is Jacamo and I have no clue whose dog he is. Anyway, what brings you around so early?"

"Half the day has gone by now if you live on a farm."

"What, 10.30 in the morning?" Isaac sounded shocked.

"Yes, but I will tell you why I have come. You are invited to Sunday dinner at my parent's farm. I have told them that you are working with me at the pub. I lied a little and said that you are a really nice man, and my mother replied that if you are all alone, I should ask you if you would like to come for dinner. She is anyways serving 14 people, one more won't make a difference. The thing is that she just can't stand the thought of anyone being alone." Summer said with a sneaky smile.

Isaac replied, "I know nothing about your parents. After meeting you and your brothers, for all I know, they could be hill-top cannibals and you are luring me up there for dinner – literally."

"Oh, thanks for that. I want you to know they haven't eaten people for about two years now since they found that beef tastes much better."

"No, joking apart..." Isaac said

"Who's joking?" Summer quickly added, "And anyway, I thought you wanted to see Beth?"

"Yes I do, but I don't want to be in her face. She probably needs time to think. It must be a really big step for her to even look at another man in that way. I don't want to rush her into anything. I know you are trying to help me Summer, but I don't think this is the right way to go about it," Isaac answered with a concerned tone.

"Well Mr. Know-it-all, it was Beth, who asked if you could come for dinner. I would have any day preferred to invite my boyfriend."

"I thought you didn't have a boyfriend?" Isaac questioned.

"I don't, but if I did..."

Isaac quickly interrupted, "It's probably that gob of yours that puts them off."

"Any man would be lucky to have me on their arm!" Summer snapped.

"Yes, until you chew it off!" Isaac laughed.

"I like you, Isaac Montgomery, you make me smile."

"I like you too, but back to the dinner, what shall I wear? A suit?" Isaac asked.

"Well if you do, you won't be allowed in. It will be like having a meal with a debt collector. No, just wear what you have on. The rest of the family will probably be wearing their work clothes and may be smelling of cow shit."

"Ok, but did Beth really ask your mum and not you?" Isaac asked sincerely.

"Yes, she did. To be honest, on the way home last night, she spoke a lot about you. She wanted to know everything about you and she was a bit like a school girl with a crush. I haven't seen her like that for years! To see her for a moment with that happiness in her eyes almost got me blubbering like a man," Summer divulged.

"Men don't cry," Isaac said.

"They do when I dump them!" Summer smiled.

"You are terrible!" Isaac sighed. "What time should I be there?"

"About 2 pm. Dinner's late today, as they are moving cattle to a new field," Summer instructed.

"Right, I will be there at 2 on the dot. Now that you're here, would you like some coffee or tea?"

"No thanks old man. I am meeting some mates at the pub."

"So, what you are saying is that your mates need a lot of alcohol to put up with you? I can understand that."

"Piss off! I'll see you at dinner and I'll tell Beth what a shit you are," Summer snarled.

"You won't, will you?" Isaac gasped.

Summer laughed and said, "Ah…got you! See you later." And with that, she made a speedy exit.

The room was in silence again.

"Well, Jacamo, I can't believe it. I'm going for a dinner with Beth and her family. I don't know whether that's good or bad. You might not believe it, but I have never gone to meet a girl's parent before. Doesn't it sound pretty serious? Do you think they are going to question me? And if they do, would I let something slip about my past? Or, am I just over-thinking everything? Perhaps it really is just a dinner for the newcomer in the village…oh for Christ's sake! I'm talking to the dog now." As if to express his annoyance, Jacayo growled. "Don't you growl at me!" bellowed Isaac. "I'm pouring my heart out to you, I fed you last night and if that isn't enough, you also slept on my bed. I can see that you and I aren't going to get on well till you realise that I am the alpha male, and this is my house. That's it now…lie on your back, you won't get any fuss from me." Jacamo followed Isaac's instructions. "Right, let's go and see what I can wear."

Isaac thought, "It's 11.30 now. I will leave around 1.30, and I should be there dead on time, or should I be a little late? Oh, for pity's sake, this is hard work! I know…I will call Pen. She'll know just what I should do."

Isaac waited patiently, while the phone rang.

"Hello Phil's phone," the voice said.

"Is that you Pen?" Isaac said, recognising the voice.

"Yes Isaac, do you want Phil?"

"No, actually it was you I was hoping to talk to. I got to speak to Beth last night and her family has invited me to dinner at their place today. The whole family's going to be there, about 14 of them. You know when I was working on the stock exchange, the figures revolved on the board with the ups and downs. When the prices were falling, I would hold firm without any panic to sell. I would just hold my nerve and wait. But the pressure of that seems like heaven when compared to this. I am actually scared to death. I haven't got a clue what I should say or do. I'm totally in a quandary. I'm really in trouble here. You have got to help me Pen!"

There was a small pause as Pen processed the information, then she answered, "Right. First, calm down. Let's talk this through. What can you tell me about her family?"

"One of her sister works with me at the pub; her two younger brothers are a pair of knob-heads and share the same brain, and…that's it. I can't think of anything else."

"Alright, we can work with that," Pen replied reassuringly. "This is how I see it going; Beth likes you but has been really hurt in her life, so they are going to be very protective of her. There is no doubt in my mind that they will throw a lot of questions at you. They will want to make sure that you have good intentions and won't hurt her. They will like to know if you are really serious about seeing her, as she hasn't had an interest in anyone for such a long time. They must be frightened that someone will come along, take advantage and then leave her. There is no doubt that she is an extremely strong woman, but how much is she expected to endure? So tell me, Isaac, are you really sure in your heart that this is what you want? Once you go down this road, there will be no turning back, and mark my words, if you do that, I will personally kill you! That's apart from what the family will do to you". She paused and then said, "By the sound of it, it seems that you have been given a chance of real love, and if you blow this you really will be dead inside. Isaac Van Horn, the stockbroker! You have changed so much over the past few months, you seem to have found real emotion, and you are growing as a person and it seems that you have already found your soul mate. This is the biggest deal you will ever make.

Just be you, the new you, and mean every word you say. I can understand that for now, you don't want them to know about the money, but tell them in no uncertain terms that you will always look after their daughter, no matter what. That is all they would want to know and you must put their minds to rest about you and Beth."

"What if it turns out that she doesn't want me?"

"Then it just means that she has come to her senses and had a lucky escape." Pen laughed. Isaac wondered for a moment whether she was being serious.

"Don't worry, I am only joking," Pen said. "From what you have told me, it seems that she does really like you. She is probably having feelings for someone once again, after years of being alone. Believe me, Isaac, that's real."

"Thanks ever so much Pen! I really do feel a lot easier about it now. I know how I feel and I must let her family know that."

"Ok Isaac, but put mine and Phil's address in your coat, in case they don't believe you and beat you to death. And don't worry, we will see to it that you have a good funeral," Pen joked.

"When did you get a sense of humour?"

"I always had! You were just too full of yourself to notice," Pen replied.

"Point taken. Shit, we've been on the phone for three-quarters of an hour. I'll give you a call later and let you know how it went. See you, and thanks again Pen. Oh, and tell Phil he is a tosser," and with a laugh, Isaac put down the phone.

Standing in his small cottage lounge, Isaac thought. "Right, I feel a bit better now. I am just going to be myself."

"What are you whimpering about, Jacamo?" Isaac said as the dog's whimpers became louder. "You don't get to go with me. Right, let's get dressed. Clean trousers, clean shoes, my fisherman's jacket and I'm ready. Oh, where's my watch? Ah, there it is. Right dog, I have left the bolt off the little door flap thing to let yourself in and out." With that instruction and a kind glance, Isaac set off on his trek.

CHAPTER SEVEN

Meet the parents

AT 1.55 PM, ISAAC WAS standing at the gate of the McCoogan's farm, taking deep breaths. He was unable to move his legs. "Right, on the count of ten, I will make my way towards the door," Isaac told himself. As he approached, the door opened.

"Hello Isaac," a kind-faced woman at the door said. "Come in, you silly boy, and call me Moragg," she instructed.

Isaac took a step back and then replied, "Oh, thank you."

"Don't be silly, everyone is in the dining room, just down the hall on the right."

As Isaac walked down the hall he thought, "Jesus, this is like walking over hot coals." Those few steps to the door of the dining room seemed to be getting further away. The door flew open and Beth was there.

"Hello Isaac, don't be shy, come on in. You can sit between me and Summer. Just make yourself comfortable."

Isaac sat hesitantly, trying not to make eye contact with anybody in the room. The dinner went really well. Everyone was mainly discussing farm business and ideas to enhance their turnover. The food was absolutely delicious and Beth seemed really talkative and friendly when Summer wasn't butting in – bless her. After dinner, everyone seemed to mingle in the living room, while Moragg rushed around busily cleaning, bringing cakes, drinks and so on.

Beth and Isaac were talking, when Moragg finally came over and said, "Beth, why don't you take Isaac for a walk around the farm. I have heard he likes to walk."

"Would you like that?" Beth asked as she looked at Isaac.

"Oh yes, definitely," Isaac replied, trying not to show his enthusiasm. Isaac thought, "I just need to get out of this place to re-group. The first stage is over." He sighed under his breath. Isaac was sure that shortly after the walk, the interrogation would start. He just knew it. As they stepped outside, he noticed that Jacamo was sitting by the gate.

"Oh, isn't that the dog that you have adopted?" Beth said glancing at the dog.

"Yes, that's him! He follows me everywhere and we don't even get along. We met for the first time last night," Isaac replied.

"Well, he obviously likes you. Animals can sense whether a person is good or bad, so I am going to say you are a good man."

They walked for what felt like hours to Isaac. Beth told him all about the farm's history, what they did, the livestock they reared, and the generations of her family that had cared for the land. Isaac talked about how beautiful it all was in this part of the world and how quiet it was compared to the city. They sat for a while on some rocks, overlooking the ocean, with the sun glistening across the waves and the gentle lapping of the sea on the shore.

Isaac mustered all of his courage and asked Beth, "I don't mean to be forward, but I was wondering if we could spend more time together. When I saw you for the first time, about three months ago with your mother at the Dipping Tank, I would admit I was quite smitten. This had never happened to me before…ever! I can remember that day quite vividly. I had to quickly leave after seeing you." Isaac then sat hopefully waiting for Beth's response.

Beth replied, "I remember that day, and know that you left quite quickly after I saw you."

"Oh, you noticed me? I thought you had just looked straight through me."

"No, I felt something too, when I saw you," Beth replied shyly, "…but my life has been very complicated over the past few years. There are things that you don't know about my past."

Isaac interrupted, "I know what happened with your husband and son…and, how it almost destroyed you."

The look in Beth's eyes suddenly changed, as she responded, "Did Summer tell you?"

"No," Isaac quickly replied, now fearing what may follow.

"Oh, I am so angry!" Beth said through gritted teeth, as her demeanour changed.

Isaac tried to explain, "No, it wasn't Summer. It was through a couple of gossip mongers, who I heard one night at the pub."

"So you felt sorry for me, is that what it is?"

"I knew nothing of this when I first saw you! It was just you and I was knocked for six." By this time, Beth had started to cry. Isaac said, "I would sooner rip out my heart than upset you! There are a lot of things you don't know about me. I have pushed women and friends away all of my life. I was a horrible man in my past. I was selfish and had to have everything and nothing was ever enough. Then one day it hit me like a bullet from a gun; I wanted to find someone special and lead another way of life. I have no clue what brought me to this place, but everything seemed right here. I wanted to find Isaac Montgomery first but then I saw you and I knew I was home. I don't even know how you feel about me. I am just hoping with all my heart that when you find out more about me, you feel that I am the person you want to spend your time with, and if you don't, it will probably be the life's way of punishing me for my past. Please, Beth, talk to me." There was a long silence as they just sat there on the rocks looking out into the sea. Isaac could hear his mind telling him, "She's too good for you, you have blown it and after what you have told her, what do you expect?"

Beth eventually said, "I do want to get to know you better, and I know the feelings that you are telling me about. I felt them last night, as I watched you work. But, you must realise that it has been a long time since I have had any feelings for a man and I know my family thinks that I should just get on with my life. But, I had dearly loved one man in my life and never thought I would ever find anyone else, or would even want someone. Davey and Little Mack were my whole life and completed me but unfortunately, they were taken away from me. For a long time, I wondered what terrible things I must have done that I had to suffer this unspeakable punishment. I decided that I would never love again, because if something like this ever happened again, I would not be able to bear it. I came to terms with the fact that the love I had been given once in my life would have to be enough to see me through to the end of my life, and I believed in it…until I saw you on that fateful day. I once more felt the warmth in my body that I couldn't explain, but it was so uplifting that I knew that I wanted to know more about you. So, it feels as if both of us owe it to ourselves to see where it leads, and I hope for the both of us that it is a good thing."

Isaac quickly answered, "We can take it as fast or slow as you feel comfortable with. I promise I will never push you into anything, you are not completely happy with. I want you to know everything about me, to be able to share your true feelings when you're ready."

Just then, she leaned across and kissed Isaac, just a gentle kiss on the lips.

Then Beth remarked, "We should get back, I think my father will want to have a chat with you."

"I know," said Isaac. "I sort of expected that, and I know why. You don't take someone so special for granted. If I am not sincere in your father's eyes, I would deserve whatever I have coming to me. So, I'll sit patiently and let him have his say because I know I'm not going anywhere unless you change your mind, which I hope you never do."

Something caught Beth's eye, "Isaac," Beth said, "You know your little dog has been sitting behind that rock?"

"No, I didn't," Isaac replied with a puzzled look on his face. "But I haven't got a clue why he keeps following me."

"What are you going to do with him?" Beth questioned.

"Well, if he wants to stay with me, he is more than welcome. I like him around, but I think he is his own boss and he will just probably leave one day."

"I think you underestimate him, he sees something in you and I think you will become great friends." Beth smiled endearingly.

Isaac said, "Most of the time I can barely look after myself, let alone another mouth to feed. Well, if he can live on microwave dinners, we should be ok. Right, we better get back to the farm, where I can face the inquisition."

As soon as Beth and Isaac walked through the door, Beth's mother shouted from the kitchen, "Come and help me with the dishes, Beth. Isaac can go and sit in the living room with your father for a minute."

Isaac looked at Beth with a flash of fear, and she smiled to reassure him. "Good luck," she said.

"Thanks, I will need it." As he walked into the living room, Beth's father was standing by the giant fireplace. The fire was fiercely burning and Isaac thought to himself, "Is it hot in here or is it just me?" There he stood, 6 foot 4 inches tall, heavily set, not an ounce of fat, or maybe just a bit round by the stomach. He had solid muscular arms, and a moustache as big as a ferret on his face.

He turned to Isaac and said, "SIT." Isaacs's legs just buckled and before he knew it, he was sitting. "Right, I won't beat around the bush. What are your intentions towards my daughter?" he bellowed or at least, it sounded like he did.

Isaac considered himself quite lucky, as he was afraid that the entire family would be in there to interrogate him. He had imagined a big long table, with himself sitting on a stool, right in front of it. "Well sir, I have real feelings for Beth and I promise I will never do anything to make her unhappy, as long as she wants me."

"What's that supposed to mean?" Big Mac grunted.

"It means I see a future with her if she will have me."

"Have you been married before?"

Isaac swore in his own mind because as Big Mac was talking in his concerned way, the vibrations from his voice echoed and bits of ceiling plaster were falling off throughout the room.

Isaac replied, "No, I have never been married. I have just always concentrated on work."

"You swear?" Mac eyeballed.

"At least for the majority of the part..." Isaac said with a grin.

"What?" Big Mac snapped.

"No, nothing. I was just trying to be funny."

"Well, I'm not laughing, am I?"

"No sir, you are not," Isaac replied in a serious tone. "And yes, I swear I have never been married."

Mac looked puzzled. "At your age, you have never been married? I was married to Mrs. McCoogan by the time I was 17 and Beth was married at 19, so what's wrong with you? Are you one of those 'love them and leave them' types?"

"No sir," Isaac replied, "I just pursued a career."

"What, to end up a barman?" Mac questioned.

"I wasn't always a barman," Isaac said with a smile. "In London, I worked in a bank."

There was a short pause as Mac took in the information that had been provided. Then he replied, "If anything comes of you and Beth, how would you support her?"

Isaac replied quickly, sticking to the story he had told. "I have some savings, plus a trust fund that matures shortly, and I will always work and look after Beth. I promise you this."

"Don't try and pull the wool over my eyes! You city folk are born to lie."

"I can assure you that my intentions are completely honourable, and yes, a lot of people are liars, but you don't need to come from the city to be one. I don't know the future, but I think we have found something that we would like to explore and see where it takes us, and I just hope you believe that to be true and that I will support your daughter forever."

"Is it your intention to take Beth to London?" Mac asked with a worried look in his eyes.

Isaac explained, "No. I wouldn't want to settle permanently in London. Occasionally, maybe I would visit my parents and would like Beth to accompany me if we are married later. I also have a sister and a brother."

"And what do they do?" Mac interrupted.

"My sister is a solicitor in Knightsbridge and my brother is one of The Queen's National Guards at Buckingham Palace. My mother and father are very well to do and are semi-retired now."

"So what happened to you? You must be a disappointment to them?" Mac barked.

"No sir, they would have to give a damn for that. That is a whole other story," Isaac said trying to change the subject.

"Well, I've got time," Mac said

"No, I mean no disrespect sir, but I don't feel I know you well enough for that, and for now it's quite personal."

"So you are the black sheep of the family?" Mac shrugged.

"If that's what you wish to believe, then so be it."

Mac then answered with a very forceful tone, "Do you know the consequences if you hurt Beth?"

"No, but I can imagine."

"No, not the consequences you will face, although they will be there as well. My concern is do you realise how upset she will be if you do something wrong? And she doesn't deserve that after all that she has gone through." Mac looked worried.

"No sir, that is the last thing I would ever want to do, and I don't know how I can I convince you of that," Isaac said, looking Mac straight into the eye.

Mac's body language suddenly changed and his voice grew softer and less intimidating. "I love my daughter, son, and if this is what she wants, then we have no choice but to allow her to try and find the right man in you. But always remember, if you do turn bad, I will kill you and serve the time for doing it."

Isaac thought for a minute then remarked, "I believe you."

"Then we understand each other?" Mac replied.

"Yes sir, we do."

"By the way, my name is Mac, not sir, so use it."

"On that note, I will say a good day, for now, Mac," Isaac said as he walked towards the door. As Isaac reached the door he turned back and stared at Mac and said, "It has been good to clear the air." And he walked out of the room.

Isaac was feeling both angry and sad at the conversation with Beth's father. But he also understood why he had to ask all the questions that he did and he wasn't sure if he could have handled it any better. Perhaps given him a bit more confidence. Isaac thought to himself, "Oh balls, I'll just have to prove to him that I am serious about Beth!"

As Isaac walked towards the front door, he popped his head into the kitchen. "Thank you Moragg, it was a lovely meal. I'm glad you invited me."

Beth looked concerned, as she remarked, "How did you get on with Dad?"

"Well, he spoke his mind and I respect him for that."

"He didn't put you off, did he?" Beth sounded worried.

"To be honest, I wish I had had a father like that when I was growing up. The one who tells you that the most important thing in life is the truth."

With that, Beth stood up from the table and walked across to Isaac. "I'll see you to the gate." She placed a hand on his arm. Isaac bid goodbyes and thanked everyone, and walked towards the door with Beth. He turned to Beth and said, "I have loved our day and our walk, and I look forward to my next kiss."

Beth pulled Isaac close and said, "Then you can have that now." And on the threshold of the door they embraced and she kissed him, but just for a little longer this time. For Isaac, it was a perfect end to the day! He turned to Beth and said, "Thanks for the lovely day," as he was lingering for the feeling to last. He turned to his shabby little companion, "Come on Jacamo, let's go home." With little happy skips as he walked, Isaac proceeded towards his cottage. Jacamo just looked up to him as if to say, "You're nuts." Isaac smiled. He did feel a bit light-headed.

CHAPTER EIGHT

Bad news

BACK AT THE FARM, AS Beth came back in the kitchen, her mother was standing there with a smile on her lips and a twinkle in her eyes.

"I've just seen Isaac out, Mum. He was thanking you again for the dinner."

"Yes," Moragg said. "I saw you in the doorway." Her eyebrow rose.

"Oh, Mum!" Beth shook her head, feeling her cheeks reddening. "So, tell me, Mum, what do you think of Isaac?"

"Well, he is certainly a good looking man with very good manners. He didn't seem to talk a lot at the dinner table, but I suppose he was a little outnumbered by us all. More to the point then, what do YOU think of him?" Moragg said as she stroked Beth's hair.

"I really like him. He makes me laugh, he listens to what I have to say, he is such a gentleman and he really accepts me for who I am. I don't have to pretend to be anyone else."

"It's good that you have been able to find someone you like. You have been on your own for such a long time, and that too not because you had a lack of suitors, but because you spurned them all. Then, this Isaac comes along and I'm surprised that you are suddenly with the fairies on cloud nine. What is it that you find so special about him?" Moragg asked. "I'm not saying I don't like him, I just want to know what you see happening with you both? Are you serious, or just friends?"

Beth looked at her mother with a small tear rolling down her cheek. "I think I want more, at least I see the possibility. I want to see in time if we can have a life together. I know it is too early to think something like that, but I sense something really special between us and I want to see it through."

"Well Beth, you know why your father and I worry about you, but if it is what you want, you know we are both here for you, whenever you need us." Moragg looked towards the door. "Oh talk about the devil and he will appear," she said as Big Mac walked into the kitchen. "Are you okay Dad? How was your chat with Isaac?"

"Well, he certainly wants to go out with you and he makes no bones about that. He also feels a great amount of affection for you, but he speaks of his parents like there is some sort of rift in his family. I can't make my mind up whether it troubles him or that's just the way it is. The man himself seems sincere enough, and on certain things, he will stand his ground. He is also not a namby-pamby, although he has got that horrible English accent. I also warned him what I would do to him if he hurts you."

"Oh, Dad." Beth sighed.

"No, but that is the best part. He just said, 'I understand and I respect what you are saying.' So against my better judgement, I think I like him. Only a piece of advice - be careful. I don't want to see you hurt again. You're too precious for me and your mother."

Beth smiled and replied, "Oh, you big romantic!"

Mac turned to Moragg, "I'll have a cup of tea." As he sat at the kitchen table getting comfortable, Mac looked at Beth and said with concern.

"Are you really sure you want this man in your life?" When Beth's gaze fell to the table, he said, "Oh, alright I'll have my tea. I have said enough for today. In fact, don't worry about the tea. I will go and check on the boys in the top fields moving the cattle."

Moragg looked at Beth, "He's running away, literally! Your father doesn't deal with feelings very well, but that's just the way your grandmother has brought him up; the wicked old witch that she is. So Beth, tell me, when are you seeing him again?"

"I will see him again on Tuesday. I will go to the pub with the boys as he is working with Summer that night."

"Well remember, treat them mean to keep them keen." Moragg chuckled.

"Is that what you did with Dad?"

"No, it was your grandmother who did that. I just picked up the pieces and moulded him back to the way I wanted him."

***

Meanwhile. Isaac was half way back home, with Jacamo closely trotting behind him. "Well Jacamo, I think that went quite well. That, my boy, is the woman I am going to marry and I don't want any arguments from you."

Isaac laughed aloud and thought, "Here I go again, talking to the dog."

"Well sorry, Jacamo, but I have to talk to somebody, and you're here." Just then Jacamo decreased his pace and then sat, while Isaac continued walking down the lane, now talking to himself. Suddenly, Isaac's mobile rang in his pocket.

"Hello," Isaac answered.

"Hi Isaac, this is Pen."

"Oh hello, Pen," Isaac replied.

"So how did it go? Phil and I have been pacing," Pen asked eagerly.

"How did what go?" Isaac acted as if he didn't know what the call was about.

"Dinner at Beth's house, you moron!" Pen snapped.

"Oh, that? It was really nice, and the roast beef was lovely," Isaac said mischievously.

"So what is her family like and were all of them there?" Pen enquired.

"Yes, they were all there. I didn't get to talk much, it all seemed so hustle bustle with everybody passing the dishes around, serving themselves and eating. I was sitting between Beth and Summer, so I majorly spoke to them. Before I knew, the dinner was over and they were all on to their personal agenda. Beth's mother suggested that she should take me for a walk around the farm, so that's what we did."

"Oh now, the interesting bit. How was the walk?" Pen said with excitement in her voice.

"What do you mean 'the interesting bit'?"

"You going for a walk."

"I would want you to know that I do a lot of walking around here. I haven't even bought a car since I have been here and have also sent the hired car back."

"Well, in that case, I think you're boring," Pen remarked. "This was a big day for you, meeting her parents."

Isaac then went on to explain the day, including Mac's stern words and how lovely Beth's mother was.

"As I was saying before I was rudely interrupted," Isaac continued, "we walked for about a mile and we sat on some rocks overlooking the sea. It was a stunning place. We talked for a while and eventually we got onto her past and mine and then I opened my big mouth and said that I had heard what had happened to her years before. She was so angry to find out that I knew about her past and she started to cry. I didn't know what to say. She thought I had just felt sorry for her and that's why I was there."

"Crikey, what did you say?" Pen said.

"She was silent for a while and we sat for about 20 minutes. I began to pour my heart out about my past and what sort of person I had been. I said that though I know that I was not a nice man, but the last thing I wanted was to hurt her, and my feelings are as real as they could be. I wanted to be with her and I knew nothing of her life when I saw her for the first time."

"So what did she say?" Pen asked.

"She said nothing, she just leaned and kissed me. I'm not kidding Pen, I had to turn away. I thought I was going to cry. It was fantastic, my heart was pumping and my whole body was trembling," Isaac explained.

"Yes, it sounds like you are in love Isaac!"

"Is that really what love feels like?"

"If you're lucky," Pen replied. "I must admit Phil has trembled some nights, but that is usually after a good curry if you know what I mean!"

"Oh Pen, what are you like!"

"Well Isaac, it sounds like you're in for the long haul then. I think it's only a matter of time. By the way, your father has been trying to get hold of you."

"Ok. Did he say what he wanted?" Isaac asked.

"No, but it sounded quite urgent."

"I will have to call him later, reluctantly, though. I'm sure he just wants to lecture or something."

"I think that would be a good idea," Pen said. "Anyway, I will speak to you soon Isaac, I'm really happy for you. Stay safe and I will look forward to some more gossip. Bye for now," Pen said as she ended the call.

Isaac continued along the lane.

"Well dog, I wonder what my father wants. Dog? Where's he gone?" Isaac could just see Jacamo about 100 yards along the lane, trotting ahead.

"Oh thanks, now you are ignoring me. Right, back home we go. I better call my so-called parents."

Isaac arrived home, made himself comfortable and decided to call home.

"Hello Dad, is that you?" Isaac said as the phone was answered.

"Oh, so you decided to call at last!"

"I have just got the message," Isaac replied. "Is something wrong?"

"Yes, your mother is dying!" Howard blurted in a callous manner.

"What do you mean she is dying?" Isaac snapped.

"Just what I said," Howard responded.

"But why didn't you tell me before? Why wait until now, how long have you known?" Isaac questioned.

"Let's put it this way. I have only got in touch with you, as your mother requested I call you."

"But why now?" Isaac asked.

"I have just told you, are you stupid?" Howard barked.

"Well, how long has she been ill?"

"For a couple of years now," Howard answered.

"And only now you decided to call me?" the outrage in Isaac's voice was very evident. "What is wrong with you, you heartless bastard?"

Howard replied, "Come or stay, I don't care what you choose. Your mother wants to see you, not me!"

"Is she at home or in the hospital?" Isaac asked.

"She is here at home. Do you remember where that is?"

"Yes!" Isaac snapped. "I would say it has been nice talking to you, but it hasn't!"

"Don't delay, the doctors are saying your mother hasn't got long. A couple of days at most."

"Don't you care at all? She is your wife!" Isaac remarked angrily.

"Like I said, she wants to see you, not me."

"I will get a flight and should be with you by mid-day tomorrow. Then we will have it out, once and for all." Isaac slammed the phone down and immediately called

"Hello, is that the airport? I need your earliest flight to Gatwick tomorrow."

"We have a flight at 10:30 am. There is one seat left on Flight 76741 to Gatwick."

"Can you book it for me under the name of Isaac Montgomery?"

"Ok, Mr. Montgomery, your flight has been booked for 10:30 am tomorrow from Glasgow Airport. We look forward to seeing you, sir. Goodbye."

Isaac put down the phone and immediately called Beth.

"Hello, this is Summer."

"Hello Summer, this is Isaac. Can you put Beth on the phone, please? I haven't got her number yet."

"Sorry Isaac, she is up to the top field with Dad," Summer replied.

"Please, can you ask her to call me? Can you tell her my mother has been taken ill, so I have to go back to London and I will call her as soon as I know what is going on."

"I hope everything is OK, Isaac," Summer said caringly.

"Thanks, Summer. I will be in touch soon." With this, Isaac put the phone down and thought, "Right," Isaac thought, "next job I must get hold of a taxi for in the morning to take me to the airport."

"Hello, is that Mr. Fitzpatrick Taxis? This is Isaac from the last cottage on the right."

"Hello, how can I help you, Isaac?"

"I need you to take me to Glasgow Airport at 5 o'clock in the morning?"

"Do you have any idea how much that will cost you, as it will be double time?"

"I need to get home URGENTLY!" Isaac snapped. "Can you do it?"

"Don't worry. I'll be knocking on your door at 5 am, Isaac."

Isaac expressed his thanks as he started to calm down. Then as the phone call ended, he turned his attention to other matters, like packing a bag. Isaac began to panic a little as though, his thoughts had very little to do with his parents, but it was still all that he knew. He was apprehensive of what may receive him. His mother had never before expressed strong feelings towards him, but know she was asking to see him…and she was dying! He felt he had to get closure and discover why they had never seemed to want him before. He had always made sure that he doesn't ask for anything until he comes of age and is able to stand on his feet. He, then, started to make his own way into the world. As for his so-called brother and sister, he hadn't spoken to them in over 20 years. He didn't even know where they lived or their phone numbers – although he had never really felt their absence. "Right," he thought, "I am all packed. I will set my alarm and try and get some sleep."

Just as Isaac started going upstairs, there was a knock on the door. Isaac opened the door and to his amazement, it was Summer and Beth.

"Please come in, I have just finished packing," Isaac said, still stunned.

"What has happened? Are you alright?" Beth said concerned, as she reached and squeezed his hand.

"I don't know. My mother is dying and has been ill for quite a long time, but nobody informed me. I spoke to my so-called father, and he tells me that she has only got days to live." Isaac could not hide the sad look on his face, as he explained.

"Oh, I am very sorry Isaac! Is there anything I can do for you…you only have to ask?"

"I have only known you for a short time, but I am totally in love with you! When I get back, I will explain everything to you."

Beth looked into Isaac's eyes as she paused, searching for a response.

"No, I wouldn't put you through that, I don't suppose it will be pleasant. It is something I need to do alone. I need answers."

Beth turned to Summer. "Thank you for bringing me down here. You get yourself off home. I'll be along later." She gestured towards the door.

"Are you sure?" Summer said, quite surprised.

"Yes," Beth replied.

"Ok, I will see you later. I will tell Mum and Dad where you are and explain what has happened."

"Thank you, sis," replied Beth.

Isaac gestured, "You don't have to stay."

"I want to…would that be ok?" Beth snapped.

"Thank you." With that Summer left after giving Isaac a reassuring hug and glancing at Beth. "Isaac," Beth said, "I know you are troubled by all of this and I get the feeling it is not your mother. There are other things going on in your life that I know nothing about. When you are ready, I am sure you will tell me." With that, Beth put her arms around Isaac's shoulders and cuddled him.

"For tonight, I just want to hold you and let you know that I am here for you always."

"I am sorry, Beth. There are some things, I just need to know before I am ready to tell you."

"Come and sit with me on the sofa, Isaac," Beth said as she gently rested his head against her shoulder and gently stroked his hair. She whispered quietly into his ear, "Everything will be ok. I will always be here for you, just know that and let it guide you back to me. So, irrespective of whatever you have to face, please know that there is someone that love you most dearly. It has been but a short time, you and me, but I like you. I just know we will be together. You are a good man, Isaac Montgomery."

Isaac just looked longingly into her eyes and slowly drifted off to sleep, knowing he was in the arms of an angel, and for the first time, he felt safe and loved. He felt that everything might be ok and he could face anything as long as he could get back to Beth.

At 4 am the alarm buzzed. Isaac slowly maneuvered himself out of Beth's arms, trying not to disturb her. She was soundly asleep and he didn't want to wake her. He got himself together as quietly as possible. He wrote a note thanking Beth and explaining that he has left quietly as he didn't want to wake her. He gently kissed her on the lips and opened she her eyes for the briefest of moments and then closed them once more. Isaac was torn between going and staying, but he knew that he needs to face his past and get some idea as to why his life had been so empty. Only then, perhaps he would truly be free to live his life, whatever it may be; free of regrets and influence of parents that he had never really known.

CHAPTER NINE

Secrets Revealed

HE REACHED HIS PARENT'S HOUSE at 12.30 pm that day, the big sprawling Montgomery Manor he had no fond memories of from the short time he had lived there. It was a house of many rooms, but with no laughter in its walls. A place where two people lived, but seldom met. The house, however, was filled with an array of people to tend to various needs. It was a beautiful royal exterior encasing imprisoned tortured souls and keeping secrets at bay. Isaac pondered for a while, just staring at the mighty doors, knowing that once they opened, he would enter the world he had spent so many years running away from. Now, it was too late to run. The taxi had left and he knew he would have to face this, so he couldn't walk away from it, although every fibre of his being wanted to never look back. As he stood staring, one of the curtains in the lower window twitched. Someone was watching him but didn't want to be seen. From what Isaac could remember, it was the window of his father's study. A room he was never allowed in. Just then the main door slowly opened. An old man dressed in a butler's attire said, "Mr. Montgomery is expecting you. Sir, if you would like to walk this way I will take you to him."

Isaac apprehensively entered. Once in the main hall, the house sent chills up and down his spine. Nothing had changed. The house still reeked of despair, but now death also roamed its corridors, waiting patiently for its next soul to take her last breathe. Isaac thought to himself, "I would like to think of happier times spent," but he could not recall one time he felt he belonged in this mausoleum that he once briefly resided in. Isaac paused for a moment at the portrait in the main hall that had no reference to him. He had been left out completely. As he looked at the Montgomery family portrait, he realised that the untrained eye would never have guessed that one member was missing or even existed.

"This way please, sir. The master is waiting."

"Then let him wait!" shouted Isaac. "He is your master, NOT mine!"

Isaac took one more look at the portrait and then turned to the butler and commanded, "Take me to him."

It was a somber walk to the man that had called himself Isaac's father, but Isaac had never seen him that way. As Isaac walked into the study, which was full of unread books ornamenting the shelves, he turned and there he was. This man was smaller than Isaac had remembered. Still stiff-backed and distinguished, but with a face of the chiseled rock.

"Please take a seat," he bellowed as he strolled to his desk, not making an eye contact with Isaac.

He sat down facing Isaac.

"I didn't realise this was a business meeting, Howard. Is this how you treat your son?" Isaac snapped.

"Let me make one thing clear…you are NOT my son!"

Isaac fell silent, trying to take in what had just been said.

"It is time you knew the truth," Howard barked.

"Then who is my father and why it has been kept a secret from me for so many years?"

"It was never spoken about because of the scandal that would have affected our standing in the society. Believe me, what your mother did could have finished my career back then, and our children's professions as well. Every family has a dark secret and you were ours."

Isaac sat bewildered and confused at the revelations. Then he replied. "So you let me live my whole life believing that it was somehow my fault. I was asking myself time after time what I had done that was so wrong that you didn't want or love me at all. Yes, you made sure I never went without anything, but I did go without love and that was my biggest problem. For years, I couldn't connect to anyone or build attachments with anybody. I was a self-loathing arrogant man. A lot like the man I see in you! I had more money than I could spend, I have treated people around me like dirt. The friends I did have, how they have tolerated me I will never know. All of this happened to cover a scandal to protect you? Did you ever think of what you had made me into, the kind of life you have given me? You has turned me into a man with money, but void of feelings; a fucking money making robot machine."

"Well, Isaac…I provided for you, out of courtesy for your mother. You mean nothing to me and I will take no credit for the man you became. That little gem belongs to your mother and your real father. To me, you were just a little bastard who almost cost me everything. You should be grateful you weren't in an orphanage. Now go and see your mother, then get out of my house. I don't expect to see you in my house again, and don't try to see your half-brother and sister. They will have nothing to do with you after today. What are you waiting for? Get out!"

Isaac paused for a moment, taking in the evil old man's words and then replied, "I am just wondering whether to beat you to death for what you have just said."

The colour drained from Howard's face, knowing in his arrogance that he had pushed Isaac too far. Isaac was furious and pictures were forming in his mind as to what he could do to Howard. He was completely enraged by the revelations that were so callously delivered as if he was not even worthy of sentiment or feeling.

"That's how it was," Howard shouted. "Now get out!!"

Isaac stood up, his fists clenched and his teeth bared. He had never in his life felt as angry as he did right now. He wanted to kill Howard with his bare hands. He grabbed him by the throat and began to squeeze tighter and tighter. He could see the life draining out of his worthless body; trying to cry out but in vain. Howard started to thump Isaac's arms, his last attempt at trying to free himself. Just then Beth's face appeared in Isaac's mind. Her love, their new life. He would lose everything if he killed this worthless excuse for a human being. He suddenly loosened the grip and released this man he had called father. Howard's lifeless body fell to the ground beside his desk.

"My God, I have killed him!" Panic began to fill Isaac's thoughts. Isaac then noticed that, like a cockroach, Howard was still alive. Isaac fell back into the large armchair he was seated in as the enormity of what he had just done dawned on him; he had almost destroyed his own life in a senseless act of anger. Isaac always had a bit of temper, but he always expressed it with words and not with violent actions. The butler then entered the room and saw his master lying on the floor. He immediately turned to Isaac and said, "What have you done?"

Isaac replied, "Something way overdue!"

"I will have to call the ambulance and police," the butler hissed.

"I don't think your master would like that," Isaac growled. "It would open up too many old wounds that have been gathering dust for too many years and draw attention. By all means, ask your master what he would like to do."

"Simpson," a weak voice sounded. "Put me in the chair." Howard didn't sound as confident as he slumped down into his chair. He looked at Isaac with fear in his eyes, considering how close he had come to his own demise. Isaac looked up at the butler.

"Simpson, take me to my mother please, if you will. Your master will be fine. He is too mean to die!"

Simpson turned to Howard and asked, "Are you sure you will be alright, sir?"

"Yes, take him to his mother, then come back and pour me some bourbon."

"Yes, sir. Please follow me, I will take you to Mrs. Montgomery's room."

The walk to the top of the stairs seemed endless. Isaac hadn't seen his mother in so many years. She had become very despondent of his calls of late. It seemed she had cut Isaac out of her life completely; probably because of the added pressure from Howard. But Isaac was sure that Howard would have to pay for it one day, in the destination called "hell." Howard had always dominated his wife, so Isaac didn't blame his mother. He just blamed the circumstances and that bombastic creep.

Simpson slowly opened the door. He saw Isabel's frail broken body surrounded by tubes, an array of monitors of all descriptions and a nurse by her side. The frail old lady was lying in the middle of a huge bed, which overwhelmed her with its sheer size.

"Hello, my name is Susan. I am your mother's nurse." A voice disrupted Isaac's thoughts and caught his attention. Isaac shook Susan's hand.

"Will that be all, sir?" Simpson asked.

"Yes, thank you, Simpson," Isaac replied.

"Oh, and sir?"

"Yes?"

"Well done, very well done, sir!" He smiled and then left the room, closing the door behind him.

Isaac turned to the nurse.

"Susan, how is my mother?" Susan took Isaac's arm and led him to the corner of the large room by the window.

"She is having a good day today," Susan smiled. "Are you fully aware of her condition?"

Isaac nodded to say no.

Susan continued, "Unfortunately it's a matter of time. We have already tried all the possible options but the cancer is aggressive. Our only option now is to make her comfortable. She requested to come home as she had some unfinished business to take care of."

"Yes, that will be me, I'm afraid."

"Oh, she is waking up. Try not to tire her out too much." Susan moved towards Isabel to ensure that she was not in pain.

"I am afraid there are certain things that we need to discuss. That is what I think she has been hanging on for. Could you leave us for a short while and I will call you if she needs you?"

Isabel gestured for Isaac to sit next to her bed.

Susan said with a smile, "I will be right outside"

"Thanks," replied Isaac.

Isaac then turned towards his mother.

"Mother, can you hear me?"

"Yes, Isaac I can. Help me sit up a little," she said with a sense of joy in her voice.

Isaac recalled his mother's sweet voice. However, now it seemed more liberated and tender as the chains of the past had been lifted.

"Let me look at you. It has been so long," Isabel said with a smile on her face. "You're such a good looking boy. You look just like your father. He was such a handsome man. It feels as if he has just walked into the room."

"Well that is my question, who is my father and why have I never been told of him?" Isaac inquired with a soft voice.

"Yes, I understand your restlessness, but first let me tell you how and in what circumstances we met. He was a young stockbroker like you are now. At that time, Howard was in love with two ladies. He just couldn't stop himself. He was a coming politician, as well as a stockbroker. We have already had Helen and Edward. He probably thought that the kids will keep me occupied, but I asked him for a divorce. I couldn't stand his lifestyle any longer, as he was betraying me on every occasion. Howard refused, as that would have destroyed his career in politics. Plus, if I would have pushed him on the matter, he must have made sure that I don't receive a single penny as alimony and he would have thrown me out on the streets. I couldn't bear the shame of that. As you know, your grandfather worked in the foreign office and was very highly respected within certain circles. So, when I told him about my plans, even he was not supportive. He said, "Don't you dare bring shame on our family or I will no longer consider you my daughter." My mother, although she felt pity for me, would never have crossed my father. For her, what he said was law. So what was I to do? I had to be the dutiful wife and live with a monster. This would be my curse. I had made my bed and I would have to lie in it. As time went on, it became easier as I saw less and less of Howard. I managed to keep myself busy with Helen, Edward and the upkeep of the house. Every now and then, I would be obligated to attend dinner parties, private functions, and rallies, whenever Howard stood for re-election as our local MP. He cared for nothing, expect his standing in the community and his personal desires. On the outside, he was a model father and family man, with a good head for business; just what his borough needed." Her eyes reflected the distress she must have gone through in those days.

She continued, "On one occasion, I was dragged to yet another stockholders party, where Howard's latest mistress was also invited. It was here that I met Victor, a young up and coming presence in the stock market, as you are now. Don't think I forgot you…I have quietly followed your career" She said to Isaac. "Gradually, Victor and I fell in love. From the first sight, I was hooked to Victor. He was so handsome and charismatic. He seemed to light up the room and the eyes of all the ladies would follow his every move, including Howard's mistress. Little did I know then that his thoughts that night were focused on me. As the night progressed, he slowly advanced towards me. A man that was so confident and outspoken on varied views seemed to stumble with his words, as he finally introduced himself to me. It was as if something had unnerved him. I later realised that it was my presence. I too felt bewildered by his attentions. I was overwhelmed with feelings that I had not had for many years. After that, we started meeting quite often and one night, under the influence of our head over heels love, we decided to consummate our relationship in secret. The mere thought of him sent butterflies in my stomach and made me feel young, vibrant, cared for and wanted. Our intense love affair continued for about a year and we just could not be apart any longer. We made a plan to leave together; Victor had decided that he would confront Howard and tell him of our plans. He was coming to the house that fateful evening to collect Helen, Edward and me to take us to our new life. I never thought it was possible to love anyone after being with Howard for 12 years. I thought I would never be happy again."

"So what happened to Victor?" Isaac interrupted.

"He was killed in a road accident two miles from here. He was on his way to rescue us and take us to our new lives and instead he lost his. I called him that night, as I couldn't understand why he had not come. I was devastated. Many questions were bombarding my mind - What have I done? Was he ok? Has Howard found out and warned him off? Has he been in an accident? I was at the end of my tether. I had to know. The following day, I got the tragic news from Victor's friend that he died the night before on the bypass two miles from our house when he was coming to save me from my life at Montgomery Manor and from the devil himself.

It was shortly after that, about a month later, when I started to realise that I was pregnant with Victor's baby. Up until this point, I had all but given up on life. I was inconsolable. But you gave me hope. I managed to keep it a secret until it was too late for Howard to insist on a termination. When he eventually found out he was furious! I thought he was going to kill me. Again, it wasn't me or our marriage, he was concerned about, but it was what other people would think that probably saved my life. He said that as far as anyone was to know, the baby was his. If I told anyone the truth, he would have me sectioned as a mad woman and I would lose everything, including my other two children. "I will put the little bastard out on the street where he belongs!" he said. So I had no choice, but to go along with the story. If I had crossed, Howard would have destroyed me and you! As long as I stayed with him, he would provide everything that you needed, until you could stand on your own two feet. And as long as

I had my children, I could bear this life or so I had presumed. However, that changed again when you were 5 years old. Howard sent you straight to boarding school and I was to have little or no contact with you. I have always loved you and whenever I could, I tried to help you."

"So, who was Victor, Mum?"

"His name was Victor Van Horn. Von Van Horn's elder brother."

"Oh my God! I work for my uncle and I have never known, but he has."

"When you finished the university and were looking for a job, I called Von and asked him to train you in your father's profession. Victor used to write Von. He had told him about his love for me, our situation and that I already had kids. He said that all this may create a scandal, but he would handle it and would explain it to him when he saw him next. He just asked him to be ready for some fallout. Victor never got to make that explanation as that was the night he died. Von came to see me about a month after Victor's death and told me of the letter his late brother had left him. I informed him about my pregnancy and explained what Howard had said. Von agreed to say nothing but said if I ever need anything, including help to leave Howard, I only need to call him and the arrangements would be made. Von told me that as I was carrying Victor's baby, it made me part of the Van Horn family. And Von would never waver on his promise to me. He told me that if Howard ever threatened me again, one phone call and he would be out my life forever. After you were born, I just mourned Victor and fell into a deep depression and found it hard to cope. Howard had taken you away from me almost immediately and at the time I had no strength left to fight. I just felt like dying. Howard employed a nanny with strict instructions that I was not to see you, but from time to time I would hear your cry echoing through this gilded palace. I would try to get to you, but the door was always slammed in my face. I was heartbroken that my baby had been taken away from me; my last link to Victor. I barely had the strength to carry on. It took me almost two years to fight my way back to sanity and once I did, I did everything I could to spend more time with you, whenever Howard was away. But he soon found out and moved you out of the house with a nanny, until you were old enough to be accepted at boarding school."

"But why didn't you allow Von take you away or at least get you away from Howard?" Isaac questioned.

"That was just not the way I was brought up and I still feared him. I didn't think anyone could save me. I was sure Howard would find a way to kill me."

"Do you know he didn't even tell me you were ill till yesterday?"

"It was my last wish to see you and tell you everything before I die. You now must go to Von and tell him that you know the truth. You are a part of a great dynasty, the Van Horn family. They are some of the richest people in the world. With their power, you will have everything your heart desires." Isabel was trying to be positive.

"Mother, I understand now what you went through to keep me safe and help me through this journey in this troubled world, but I have left all of that behind in search of love…and I have found it. To me, this is more powerful and satisfying than money."

"You really are just like your father. He wanted to give everything up for his love for me. I cannot turn the clock back son, but as long as I know you have your father's spirit and outlook, I know you will be happy, and that is all I have ever wanted for you! I wish I had more time to get to know you properly, but sadly my time has nearly run out. I am so tired and I long for peace and freedom from this pain, and freedom from that evil man. Always know, that I have loved you since the day you were born and that I have thought about you each day of my life!" Isabel said with tears welling in her eyes. With that, her body went limp and the light in her eyes seemed to fade as they closed.

"Mother… Mother…wake up Mother, please! It's too soon. Please, there are questions I need to ask. Please, please wake up! SUSAN!!" Isaac shouted.

Susan ran into the room immediately and checked Isabel's pulse. She tried to get a response from her until Isaac asked her to stop. "Perhaps, now she will find the peace she wanted so much."

Isabel's face suddenly looked 10 years younger now. The pain of her life seemed to have disappeared and she was finally at peace. Isaac wept for her as he held her hand, but was relieved in knowing that she was free. He hoped that Victor was waiting for her on the other side and she would, at last, be with her true love – "My FATHER!"

CHAPTER TEN

Facing the facts

Isaac took some time and composed himself. He thanked Susan for all she had done. He made his way back down the stairs. His emotions were all over the place. He wondered, why had this been held back from him by his mother and Von? It felt like everyone but he knew about this secret. He felt that he could never see Howard again because he might just kill him. He made his way to the front door and let himself out. He hadn't called a taxi; he just needed to walk and be alone with his thoughts. Whatever he knew of his world had just been snatched away from him and a new one was put in its place. The only thing he knew for sure was that he wanted to go home, which now was Corngurn, where his new life had begun.

Isaac's thoughts went back to his mother's words as she lay dying on her bed. She really did always love him. He had felt that when he had looked into her eyes. Just as Isaac had become a prisoner of his own making, with the bars holding his feelings from the world, so had his mother been imprisoned by the truth of tragically losing the real love of her life. She was compelled to give up her son...Victor's son and she had become an empty woman, who was held in captivity by her jailer, Howard. But now she was free; her penance had been done. This helped him decide that he won't be enslaved to his heritage. He decided to talk to his new so-called Uncle Von and tell him that he is done with the financial world. He thought "I want to be free to follow my own dreams. I will not be swayed. There would be nothing he could say to me that would make me change my mind." Isaac continued to walk while thinking about all that has happened - meeting his mother and for the first time actually talking to him, along with the news that she gave. Isaac was happy that he got the chance to say goodbye. Now he knew the truth. At that time, Isaac was not aware that his world would soon unfold into a story of wealth, lies, deceit, murder and all the other trappings of life that he so wanted to escape.

Eventually, Isaac took a taxi.

"Please take me to Penderton Apartments W14." Isaac had decided to stay the night with Phillip and Pen and hopefully get their view on the revelations of the day and the decisions that he had taken. First, he thought, "I must call Beth, just to allay her worries, as I had left so quickly that night". Luckily, Isaac had a quiet cabby. Isaac thought if he had been asked how he was he would have broken down in tears. Isaac's eyes were already glazed and the odd tear found its way down his cheek. Isaac could never remember feeling so low in his life, other than when he had broken down at Phillip's place. He wondered why the taxi couldn't go any faster; he was literally just holding it together. Isaac lay back and closed his eyes for a moment, trying to block out how he felt. Then the next thing he knew they were already outside Penderton Apartments. He decided to call Beth later and wondered how much he should tell Pen and Phil, before speaking to Von.

Isaac knocked on the door. It quickly swung open and there stood Pen.

"Come in you reprobate, and give me a hug," she said with a friendly smile. Isaac squeezed her tightly in his arms.

"Thank you for putting me up on such short notice," he said in a low tone as if he sympathised that she had to.

"How long are you staying Isaac?" Penny said as she closed the door behind him and welcomed him in.

"Hopefully just a night or two," Isaac replied with his head down, heavy as if the weight of the world was on it.

"Well, Phil should be back in about 20 minutes, would you like a drink?"

"Coffee please," Isaac answered.

"Oh, I was thinking something stronger, but if that's what you want, one coffee coming up," Penny said with a smile and cheeky look. "Well Isaac, don't keep me in suspense, how did it go with your father?"

Isaac fell silent for a moment and again looked at the floor, avoiding Penny's eyes in fear that she would see his pain.

"My mother died today," Isaac replied with a clear quiver in his voice. It was clear he was trying to keep it together. His eyes were now beginning to fill with tears that he could not hide. His face seemed to have been drained of colour, as he said the words as it obviously made it more real. To say it out loud was admitting the fact, while till now he had pushed it down into the depths of his consciousness.

"I am very sorry Isaac, so very sorry," Penny said in shock. The tears were now forming in Penny's eyes as she realised the severity of what he was saying and the magnitude of the situation. "Come here you big lug," Pen beckoned. "I am so sorry. There really are no words."

Isaac looked up and saw Penny's face, which again made it all too real.

"Can we not talk about it now? There are so many things I need to share with you and Phillip. I just need some time to process things. I value your opinions. You are my true friends."

Just then Philip arrived home. He did not assess the situation or notice Isaac and Penny's distress.

"Oh, look what the tide dragged in!" Phil remarked with a mischievous smile on his face.

"Phil, shut up and sit down," Penny growled as she raised her voice. "Isaac has some devastating news. Please, Isaac, say what you need to say."

Isaac composed himself, and then bit by bit told them the whole story - the revelations of the day; Howard's response towards him and his mother; the hidden story within a story; the true love, loss and persecution in his mother's life, Howard's betrayal's and cruelty; and how he would not let her go and made her a prisoner for the remainder of her life. He said that he finds solace in the fact that she finally escaped with her death and was now free of Howard. Isaac then informed them of Victor and Von. He told them that his mother had made him promise that he would go and see Von, and tell him that he now knows the truth. But, in reality, all he wants is to just go home to Corngurn and to Beth. Isaac explained how he had decided that he would confront Von the next day and tell him his mother's last words He said, "I feel it is important to her that Von knows the truth and I speak to him." Isaac decided to go and meet Von at the office the very next day; the sooner he faced him, the sooner he could get back home. Penny and Phil listened to it all with open mouths but were barely able to offer any comments, as the story and the circumstance were both very serious. They just let Isaac know they were there.

***

The next day Isaac went to the office. He was early, so he patiently waited. After a good night's sleep, he was now composed, with his business head on and calm in disposition as he waited for Von to arrive.

Just then he heard some voices from the long corridor. "Good morning," followed by, "Good morning Mr. Van Horn."

This was the same greeting that he had been hearing from the past many years at sharp 9 am from the entire staff of the company. Von would know if anyone was missing. Thirty years and he have never been late, rain or shine. "Good morning Isaac," Von bellowed as he approached Isaac. "Good to see you back. Have you sorted your problems out that you took a long time off for? Well, time's money, so good to see you back at it." Von said this without a pause and not giving Isaac the opportunity to reply.

Isaac said, "I hoped I could speak to you, Von, if you could spare the time?" He said this with determination to indicate that he was serious.

"You better come into my office then," beckoned Von as he walked past Isaac. As he entered the office and strolled to his desk, he cast a backward glance at Isaac and said, "You better take a seat."

Isaac apprehensively sat on the chair in front of Von's massive desk. Von hung his coat up and made his way to his seat.

"Right Mr. Montgomery, how can I help you?"

Isaac hesitantly replied. "My mother, I believe you know her, died yesterday." He paused. "She wanted me to tell you that I know the truth now." Isaac stared directly into Von's eyes so he could not look away.

"So you know, Isaac. Before I say anything let me say that your mother was an exceptional woman. That is why your father, Victor fell in love with her." He paused. "Unfortunately it was not to be. I am heavily saddened by this news, but life goes on. You have no idea on how many occasions I have wanted to tell you, but I respected her decision to one day tell you herself. How have you taken this?"

"It was as if my whole had suddenly changed. I could not comprehend the depths of such deceit," Isaac replied. "As the story unfolded, I realised why she was always grieving and a mess. She had no one to turn to and she had almost lost her mind when Victor died. Howard had always controlled her, but from that day the cruelty became his weapon of choice, and after 30 years from that night of passion with Victor, he would finally put her on the ground."

Isaac leaned forward with his head in his hands and gently spoke, "Why didn't you stop him, Uncle Von?"

"Your mother made me promise to never hurt Howard. She blamed herself for making him the man he had become, which is ridiculous, and she would accept his mistreatment as her punishment. She believed it was her destiny. To be true, I thought that this was a temporary feeling due to her grief, but from time to time when I spoke to her she would always say, 'Remember your promise, never hurt Howard.' She promised one day she would tell you of your father…my brother." Von paused for a moment and then continued. "What your mother never realised was that Howard has always been rotten to the core and no matter what her decision would have been, he would have always been cruel. But I know one thing for a fact, according to my contacts at the bank, he will soon see his world crumble around him. I spoke to your mother about this and said that for her own protection, she should sign everything over to a loved one, in case anything should happen to her. Isabel signed it all over to you. Of course, Howard was too busy with his life of womanising and being the big man, constantly in control, or so he thought. In his arrogance, he never realised that even his prisoner of cruelty could have her financial revenge."

"But what of my brother and sister, when was the last time you spoke to them?" Isaac said as he thought to himself.

"I actually can't remember, because they despised you just like Howard," Von replied in an angry voice. "You were Isabel's dirty secret to be shown and shamed. Well whatever you decide, your future lies here. After all, you are a Van Horn now and that automatically makes you a partner. I can't believe how much you resemble Victor. You are cut from the same cloth and he would be so proud of you."

Isaac just sat with disbelief on his face.

Von then started to say, "Wait until you meet the rest of the family."

Isaac quickly answered, "It's a lot to take on at the moment. I don't know if I am coming or going. I need time to collate all the information

I have been given and accordingly make a plan to move forward. Do you remember when I left a few months ago? It was because I was facing a crisis in my life. I suddenly wanted more than just the endless pursuit of money. I was amassing so much money, I loved and breathed the stock market, but it did not make me happy. It just made me ruthless and hollow. I will never know why or how some of my friends decided to stay friends with me. I started to see that I wanted what they have…each other. I also wanted to be like them - planning families and futures." Isaac paused, again holding his head in his hands. The weight felt tremendous. "This is why I went away. To look for a new life and a woman to share that life with. To actually introspect, if I was capable of loving one person, other than myself. And I am happy to say that I have discovered I can."

Isaac fell quiet as he gave Von time to take in what he had just said.

Von went quiet for a moment, deep in thought, then he lifted his head and said, "And you think living on backwaters in Scotland, working in a bar for a pittance, and by having a relationship with one pretty girl, who has problems of her own is going to make you happy? Would living in a dirty old cottage fulfill your life?" By the time he reached the end of his statement, Von was bellowing.

Isaac was considering his words and the tone. He replied, "How do you know all this?" The shock was apparent in his voice.

"You don't understand, but you will. You are my nephew. I need to keep you safe. There is always someone watching over you and this has been so your entire life. You are my brother's son and heir... you are a Van Horn! And whether you like it or not, this is your legacy. Victor died, so you became my responsibility and my family. We are a proud family and we look after our own."

Isaac pondered Von's words. "Does that mean you will not allow me to make my own decisions and go back to Scotland and live my life as I please?"

Von fell silent as he carefully picked his words to respond to Isaac. "I understand your confusion, and what you feel you want. Your father had the same thoughts when he fell in love with your mother. So go and find what you are looking for - start a family, but always remember that there is a place for you here and a family that would really like to know you better." Von sounded sincere as he spoke in a mellow manner.

"What of the person spying on me?" Isaac inquired.

"I assure you that you would never see him, but he would always be there," replied Von, looking very serious. "Your connection to the Van Horns makes you a target for our enemies."

"But nobody knows. I am Isaac Montgomery, who is not related to you. I am just a stockbroker who worked here at Van Horns." Isaac looked concerned and confused. "I thought it was a big secret."

"Believe me, nephew, somebody always knows. That's the curse of being a Van Horn, and having such a successful firm. Anyone who can hurt us or extort money from us will, and they won't care how they do it. Didn't you ever wonder why I'm considered so ruthless against our competitors? It's how I protect my family. One sign of weakness to anyone and the vultures would descend upon us and a tragedy will be our only reward." Von went quiet for a moment. "That it is why your father was killed; it was a botched kidnap attempt, but believe me the people responsible for that are no more, and that's all you need to know." Von scowled.

"But my mother said it was an accident," Isaac said with confusion on his face.

"That is what was reported by the press. It was all kept very quiet in the interests of the family and the firm. It would have profoundly impacted the stock market of the day. Damage limitation protocols were put in place as directed by the shareholders for controllability, so there would be no loss of confidence in the Van Horns," Von explained.

"But you never told my mother...why?" Isaac asked.

"Your mother was very fragile at the time. It was better that she thought it was an accident. I hoped that she would be able to handle that better instead of murder. I think I made the right decision and I'll stand by that."

Von pondered for a moment and then looked at Isaac for his opinion. "No I understand that and thank you, but this changes everything."

"In what way Isaac?"

"I have found somebody as you know; for me, she is the one I have fallen in love with. The moment I saw her, it hit me like a bolt of lightning; she was the one. But now from what you have told me, I could be putting her life in danger by just being with her. How could I do that to someone? She is an innocent in this game we chose to play, yet I would live a life with torment without her. I have never felt this way before. It is joy, sadness, longing, a piece of myself that I cannot live without. What am I supposed to do?"

Von's answer was clear "Tell her the truth, everything, and let her decide for herself. If she feels the same as you do, she will be there for you. If she doesn't, you must let her go!"

"Thank you Von, but you don't know her."

"I'm sorry Isaac, but I really do," Von remarked. "I know everything about her husband and son who lost their lives at sea, the way you met her, her family's past and present. I have to know everything, it's how I keep us safe."

Just then Isaac's phone rang, "Oh hello, Beth," Isaac answered. "I'm sorry I haven't called you. I was meaning to, but so much has been happening here."

"How is your mother?" Beth inquired.

"I'm afraid she died," Isaac replied with sadness in his voice. "About an hour or so after I came. We had really talked for the first time. But even in that time, I learned so much that I need to come to terms with. Let's just say it's complicated for now. I will explain it to you when I see you again."

The call went quiet for a moment and then Beth asked, "Would you like me to come to London for a bit of moral support?"

"I really think I would like that," replied Isaac. "I'll tell you what Beth, I'm in a meeting at the moment. I will call you later and we will make the arrangements." Isaac said goodbye, biting his lip, so as not to sound mushy in front of Von.

Von looked at Isaac, pondered for a moment and abruptly said, "You must tell her the truth. You cannot live with a lie. She sounds like she can put up with a lot of things but not a liar."

"I know. But the problem is I have started our relationship with a lie. When I first went to Corngurn and people asked, I just said that I used to work in London as a bank teller. I said that I saved some money to take a much-needed break and came to Corngurn to decide what I wanted to do with my life. And like so many lies, I have backed myself into a corner and now I don't know how to find a way out." A realisation of what he had done suddenly hit Isaac. "All Beth wants is her barman that works at the local pub and lives in the last house on the right."

"You must bring her here and tell her the truth," Von sternly said to Isaac. "If she loves you as much as you say, she will stand by you no matter what, but also remember that she may wish to leave and in such a case, you must accept that."

"No, I can't," replied Isaac. "I will have to find a way," Isaac said with a wavering voice.

CHAPTER ELEVEN

The truth

BETH WAS SITTING WITH HER sisters, Summer and Mary around a large kitchen table. Moragg walked in to make a pot of tea. "Right what's going on? A minute ago you all were like three hens clucking and now you go quiet as I walk in."

"Beth has just spoken to Isaac in London," Mary replied.

"Oh, is he ok?" Moragg asked.

"No. His mother died yesterday," Summer said with sadness in her voice.

"Oh, that's terrible news. Poor Isaac, he must be devastated." Moragg said to Beth, who was sitting quietly in thought. "What did he say?"

"Well, he was quite abrupt on the phone, but I think he was busy in a meeting. He said he would call me later."

"Girls, aren't there some jobs that you need to get done? I would like to speak to Beth, so away with you." She had a stern look on her face and that hint in her tone created a sense of urgency. "Right Beth, let's have a nice cup of tea and a slice of cake. That always makes stuff better," Moragg smiled. "Beth, how do you really feel in your heart about Isaac?" Moragg tenderly asked gripping Beth's hands in hers.

The answer came with water filled eyes. "I miss him terribly and it's only been a couple of days. I literally get butterflies when I speak to him. I think it's too good to be true and he's never coming back. I haven't even known him that long, just a few months, but I know I would spend the rest of my life with him. And from what he has told me, he feels the same."

Moragg squeezed Beth's hand and then wiped away the tears from her eyes. "Don't give up just yet then. He sounds like he's going through quite an ordeal at the moment and his thoughts are all over the place, but the man I met last Sunday had eyes only for you. I do believe he is smitten with you; you stole his heart and whether you like it or not he is yours. And besides that, he took a tongue lashing from your father and stood his ground for what he believed. He told your father he would do anything to make you happy and that he would never hurt you. He said he would always be there for you and that he has never had feelings for any women that could capitulate him in this way."

"He really said all that?" Beth smiled.

"Yes he did," Moragg said as she hugged her daughter. "And I believe him."

"Oh, Mom," Beth cuddled her Mom and they both shed a tear before they saw the fruit cake. By this time Beth's two sisters were back in the room as they had quietly been listening outside the door.

"Well, we weren't going to be left out when the cake was being eaten. Anyway, it's cold in that hallway," Summer snapped.

"Come on you nosy buggers and get some plates." Moragg beckoned.

***

Meanwhile back in London, Isaac returned to Phil and Pen's apartment. He let himself in. The flat was quiet; nobody was in. "Ok good," thought Isaac. "Time to think." Isaac began to ponder the predicament he had now found himself in. "What a mess!" he thought. "My life has changed so much in past couple of days." One thing he knew above all was that he wanted Beth. She was a constant to him; position, money suddenly meant very little. He was now a part of something life changing, with many implications and possible fall out that it could not be ignored. Even if Isaac wanted to, he knew Beth would not be able to live in London. She was too pure of heart for a place that never sleeps and has more crimes in one day than Corngurn has had in a lifetime. He decided that he needed to talk to her face to face.

Isaac could still not get to grips with how his life had changed so dramatically in the past two days. He decided to leave Phil and Pen's, as he was not ready to answer any questions until he could get it clear in his own mind. He wrote a note thanking them for their hospitality and let himself out. Isaac just felt he needed his own space to try and make sense of things, so he booked himself into a hotel suite and just sat there for hours, mulling over everything in his mind. Suddenly he thought, "Christ, I should have called back Beth hours ago." Isaac grabbed his phone quickly and dialed the number.

"Hello this is McCoogan Farm," a voice said. It was Beth's mom.

"Hello Mrs. McCoogan, this is Isaac. May I speak to Beth?"

"Of course. I will hand her the phone. Sorry about the news of your mother Isaac," Moragg offered her condolences.

"Thank you."

The phone went quiet for a moment.

"Hello Isaac, I was worried about you. You didn't call," said Beth with concern evident in her voice.

"I'm sorry Beth, I just had too much to sort out and get my head around the revelations I have heard over the last few days. I am so glad you offered to come to London."

"Are you sure that's what you want Isaac?" Beth asked worriedly, having never been on a plane before or out of the county.

"Oh yes my love, there are so many things I need to discuss with you."

"Then yes, I will come," replied Beth.

A smile came over Isaac's face. "Right! I will arrange everything for you - taxi, flight, booking times, etc. I will see you at the airport."

"It all seems very hurried," a concerned Beth replied.

"I'm sorry. I just want to see you and hold you in my arms once more."

Beth's heart missed a beat and a big smile appeared on her face, "Then I will see you tomorrow."

"I love you, Beth."

"I love you too, good night."

Beth pondered for a moment. Fear gripped her as she thought about the trip ahead. She had never been so impetuous in her life. This must really be love, coupled with fear, and excitement. She could not contain herself. She ran to tell her mom and dad. Beth almost fell into the kitchen. "I'm going to London!" she shouted, excitement gripping her. "I'm going to see Isaac," she said with a warm glow on her face and happiness in her voice. "Isaac's arranging everything and calling me back later with all the details."

"What do you mean going to London?" big Mac bellowed. "I forbid it and that's all I'll say on the subject."

"Oh please, Dad!" Beth cried.

"Oh, let her follow her dreams, Mac!" Moragg beseeched. "You were young once."

"Yes I was, but I was a man of the world and could handle myself. I know what it's like out there." a stern look came across his face.

"A man of the world," giggled Moragg. "The furthest you've been is Glasgow."

"Yes, but—" Mac clambered for words.

"Yes but nothing. Let her go. If she faces any trouble, she knows that all she has to do is pick up the phone and call us. I trust that Isaac will look after her." Moragg held Mac's arm and said, "She's not your baby anymore; let her fly, she has been alone for such a long time. Although she will never forget the life that she has lost and which almost destroyed her, she needs to go forward in her life." Tears were now streaming from Moragg's eyes. "She needs this. She has mourned for a long time. I feared we had lost her, and if for some strange reason fate has brought Isaac and Beth together, we must allow it to happen."

"Please say I can go, Dad. I'm 30 years old and I've never been out of the village, and moreover, Isaac needs me now." There was a sad but determined look on Beth's face as she waited for her father to reply.

Mac pondered his daughter's request and then in true male wisdom replied, "Well, if your mother thinks you should go, then so be it." With that Mac and his sons retired to the living room to watch television, while the womenfolk all went to help Beth with her packing.

There was a scurry of activity.

"You should take this."

"Put your hair up Beth, like those models you see."

"Do you want to borrow my dress?"

"These earrings will go with it."

"Oh, not those shoes."

"Do you want my sexy nighty?" Summer paraded around the bedroom with a million questions and suggestions.

"We'll have none of that," shouted Moragg. "She is a good girl."

"What are you saying, Mom?" Summer argumentatively replied.

"That's best left for another time," Moragg sternly looked at Summer. The mayhem continued with a flurry of activities until Beth was packed. "Her clothes are all neatly packed; her travel clothes are laid out for the following day; her travel money is in her bag and her emergency money is in the suitcase if she faces any trouble….all done!" Moragg checked that everything is in place.

Beth's sisters were happy for her. They were excited that she is embarking on this big adventure, but they were also a little apprehensive and frightened at the same time. They were a very tight-knit family and what affected one, affected all. "Girls, would you give me a minute alone with Beth?" Moragg sat quietly in the corner of the room, trying to think of the words of wisdom that she would share with her daughter before, she goes on to find her destiny or god forbid, face a heartbreak. Above all, she wanted her to know that they would be there for her always. Moragg gently cuddled Beth and whispered in her ear, "I hope you find what you are looking for. God knows you deserve it in your life. You have suffered way too much in such a short life."

"I love you, Mom. I will be okay." Beth and Moragg just held each other. Beth could feel the warmth of a mother's love and concern for her child.

Early next morning, after much disorganisation and driving from Big Mac, Beth managed to catch her plane on time. Isaac had called later in the night and shared with her all the travel details that were required. Before she could even finish her cup of coffee, they were already landing at Gatwick. To say her nerves were in tatters would be an understatement. Her legs were still shaking, when she came into arrivals. But then like an apparition she saw Isaac waiting for her with a smile from ear to ear. Isaac could not contain himself. He ran to Beth, lifted her off the ground, spinning her round and round, squeezing and kissing her. "Thank you for coming. You have no idea what it means to me."

Beth caught her breath. "Well, you wanted me here, so here I am! I can't believe how big London is," Beth confessed. "You know, we're still at the airport, don't you? This is over an hour away from London," Isaac laughed. "Right, Beth I have my car in car park 4. We will catch a shuttle bus," Isaac pointed.

"Is your car in London?" Beth asked naively.

"Yes," replied Isaac. "Of course not silly, it would just be a long walk."

"Well let's go," Beth gestured. "I want to see London." They arrived at Isaac's car and he started to put the luggage in the boot. "Oh, it's a sports car. Only two seats, but a lot of room." Beth looked puzzled, "What do you do when you have friends with you?"

"I use one of my other cars," Isaac explained.

"How does a barman afford that?" asked Beth.

Isaac turned to Beth. "A barman can't afford all that, but I was someone else before I met you. Things have changed drastically over the last few days and I need to tell you everything. I love you a lot."

"Isaac you are worrying me now. You're not married, are you? Because I will never forgive you if you are." Beth was shocked. She wondered what he was hiding.

Isaac quickly answered, "No, my love. It's nothing like that,"

"But it sounds like you have lied to me."

Isaac thought for a moment, "Please...please give me a chance to explain when we get to London. All I can say is that there are no other women in my life, but you."

So off they set to the city, almost in complete silence, except for the occasional word or two from Isaac about their journey – traffic and various landmarks. But not a murmur from Beth; her mind was in turmoil. "I should have gone straight home," she thought. "I can't put myself through this. The first man I have fallen for in so many years and I find out he is a liar." Beth just wanted to burst into tears. She could feel herself shaking. "I must hold it together," she thought. "Why did he have to lie to me?" an hour's journey seemed to last an eternity. Isaac continued towards London with a sad, concerned look in his eyes.

"What have I done?" Isaac thought. "God, you gave me this chance, please don't take it away from me. I love her way too much to be able to bear it." the longest journey of his life came to an end. As Isaac pulled up outside the hotel, he quickly jumped out, ran around and opened the door for Beth, leaving the concierge bewildered by the young man's actions.

"Should I take the cases up to your room Mr. Montgomery?"

"Yes, thank you." Isaac then placed a note in his hand, looking towards Beth. "Will you let me talk to you? They have a nice coffee area in the hotel and I will explain to you and you will see I am a sincere person – perhaps a little confused. But you will understand why I omitted the truth to you."

"We will see Isaac," an angry Beth answered. "We will see."

Once at the hotel, Isaac began his story as Beth listened in anticipation for the truth. He shared how he had become a feeling-less money maker; how he had no concerns about how he made it; how he would destroy people just for his own needs. He had become totally ruthless in his life. He had made millions upon millions of pounds but had been empty of emotions, feelings, humanity, and one day he just broke down in front of two of his closest friends, who for some reason hadn't given up on him. At one time, whatever Isaac wanted Isaac got - the women, the parties, gambling…the list goes on. But through it all, he realised that he didn't know how to love, and that was when he had his epiphany and ended up in Corngurn. "I didn't want to be that person anymore. I wanted to be a man that lives a full life and if that meant working in a bar or on a farm. I wanted it. I want you and I lied because I was ashamed of who I had become. I didn't want people to see me as I was, just how I am now…just Isaac."

Isaac continued his story for what seemed like hours. Beth was so weary by this time, not just by listening intently to Isaacs's life story and taking in everything but also because she was trying to come up with a conclusion about how she felt. She really did love Isaac with all her heart, but was he the Isaac she knew now and fell so hard for? She said, "I cannot think. It is all too much. I just need to lie down and rest for an hour or two. I feel so confused at the moment. Everything has been so quick. Please Isaac, if you have a room for me, let me be alone for a while."

"Sorry," Isaac said. "I just didn't realise that you must be exhausted. I will take you to your room."

"No. Please just let me have the key," Beth prompted. "I will find the room myself, just give me some time alone, Isaac."

"Of course, I will call you later."

So Beth left with the weight of the world on her shoulders. Her simple life could now be gone forever. A good sleep and a warm shower would hopefully put a new perspective on her decision. Beth opened the door to her room and was a little overwhelmed with a four poster bed, massive television, sofa, views of the city through double-glazed windows, flowers and chocolates and luxury beyond luxury. She sat on the bed and thought, "I must call Mum.' But, before she could do that, she fell asleep.

***

Meanwhile, back at the coffee shop, Isaac had to take some big decisions about his future. An extremely worried Isaac sat deep in thought imagining all the different scenarios that may occur. He was at an all-time low once more. What he wanted was to just walk away from the Van Horns for a simpler, honest and straightforward life. If he ever needed some money, he had a lot at his disposal. All ties with his family died, when his mother passed on, but now there would be this new family to consider - his blood connection to the Van Horn dynasty. Von had been very vague as to what he expected of Isaac. Now the truth had been revealed. Isaac realised how Von had guided him throughout his career. He had taken him under his wing and taken a personal interest in everything that Isaac did in his professional life. He had almost primed him to someday be as hard and ruthless, as he had become to safeguard himself and others – or was it just greed, Isaac pondered. He knew in his own mind that Von would not just let him walk away; he saw him as a Van Horn, Victor's son and heir. Isaac now understood how his life had been orchestrated and carefully planned. He was being pushed in the right direction to become a stockbroker. Isaac's memory drifted back to his mother's words; she had told Isaac that Victor wanted out of the family business and was on the verge of leaving – "escaping," as he put it – and starting life anew with her. They had spoken of earlier that day when Victor died.

Like a light being switched on, Isaac thought, "What if Von knew this? What action would he have taken to stop his brother? Could he have had him killed, his own brother? No, maybe, I am just being silly." But it was still there in his mind; there just seemed to be so many holes in this story, Isaac thought, from a badly planned kidnap attempt to the accident itself. He had done his research. Witnesses said that the road was quite slow that day; there appeared to be nothing out of the ordinary, weather conditions were good and the headlines in the papers illustrate that it was just an unfortunate accident and no one else had been involved. A complete cover up orchestrated by Von– as he put it – to protect the reputation of the Van Horns, leaving so much unexplained about what really happened that fateful night. Isaac began to recollect some of the stories of Von's ruthlessness towards the people who made the mistake of crossing him. He had the power to dismantle their lives with no conscience about the innocents that were dragged in on his revenge. It was said that one of the junior partners, primed for success, had lost money through a simple mistake and miscalculation in his figures. The next thing he knew was that he was escorted out of the building and bundled into a waiting car, never to be seen again. Isaac knew, with so many of these incidents that he had heard of, there must be an element of truth behind them.

Von had said to Isaac himself in plain words, "No one crosses Van Horns, and as times passes by, you will come to realise this." Isaac had the feeling that if he didn't comply with what was going to be expected of him, Von would rain retributions down on him, and more importantly to Isaac, on Beth. He could not believe that a few months before, he would have probably jumped at the chance of being a Van Horn. It would have got him the power, the money, and even his birthright, he thought; but none of this would have made him happy. He had become a man in a sea of grief. What he truly needed was Love.

Isaac looked up at the sky, "I am sorry Mum; I know you thought you were doing the best for me and the reasons why you could not be there. I wish I had gotten to know you better. But through all of this, I know that you love me and will be my strength while doing what must be done."

Isaac, by this time, had reached his hotel room. He lay back for a moment, his soft couch cradling him and he drifted into a deep sleep, which had resulted from the weight upon his shoulders and a very traumatic day. The thought of losing Beth had become a reality he could not bear. The following morning Beth woke up from her slumber still fully dressed. Her phone was on the floor, where it had fallen the previous night. Last day was filled with a lot of hustle bustle - catching a plane with a very irate father for the ride to Glasgow, landing and meeting Isaac, getting through London to the hotel, Isaac's revelations about who he really was. By the time Beth had reached her room, her body and mind had just seemed to shut down, and had sent her into the deepest of sleep, so that once she awakens, she would have the strength to make the right decision.

Quickly calling her mother, she apologised for not letting her know that she was ok. After her conversation with Moragg, Beth decided to freshen up and take a bath. Of course, for Beth, the massive bathroom was nothing less than a magical room, filled with coloured bottles of all shapes and sizes, perfumes, a telephone on the wall, a television and two sinks, a swimming pool, the Jacuzzi, and the hidden lights on the ceiling reflecting all of the colours of the rainbow. Beth imagined it was something out of a fairy-tale. She could not believe this place was for her to use. She explored her new surroundings, opening all the bottles, allowing a hint of each to send its essence into the room. Her bath was ready. Beth slipped out of her clothing and gently submerged into the heavenly water. The luxurious bath salts were still bubbling beneath her and sending the glorious fragrance of sensuality and calm that washed over Beth. The feelings in her heart for Isaac were also bubbling inside her heart as she replayed the scene from the day before in her mind. She had sensed the pain and the sorrow in his eyes, as he shared his life story. He had gently caressed her hand cradling it in his. He was most certainly, not the Isaac she had fallen in love with. In a moment, for Beth, he had become someone else, a stranger she knew nothing about. But she had sat through it all before her tiredness washed over her. When she could take no more, she had simply pulled away from Isaac and retired to her room, with so many feelings that she could not make sense of. Excitement, sorrow, anger, love, hope - all swirled through her mind till she dropped like a stone on her bed. But now, as she lay there in her watery heaven, she realised that Isaac had not planned any of this when he came to Corngurn. He was escaping his life that he didn't want to be a part of. As he had said, he wanted to find Isaac Montgomery and who he wanted to be. He had not come to find someone to love; he came to find a way to be true to himself in what he really wanted, and for that, he was just Isaac. But when they met, the attraction just grew.

Beth realised a life without him would be unbearable. It had been so many years of mourning – a feeling of guilt for her to fall in love again. But for Isaac, it would be like two broken souls drifting through life finding each other and becoming one whole. Life is fleeting and Beth wanted to be with her Isaac. She lay there in her solitude, remembering the first kiss and the feelings that washed over her as they sat on the rocks watching the sea gently caress the shore, while the sun slowly descended. She could still feel the first embrace of the warmth and feeling of oneness in his arms. Beth suddenly felt a gentle shiver through her body. The awareness of her were feelings manifesting themselves into a sense of arousal. In her mind, she was imagining Isaac caressing her gently, running his masculine hands through her hair and gently stroking and holding her, sending warm feelings of desire cascading throughout her. She began to gently run her hands over herself, eyes tightly closed as her imagination took command. Warmth and feelings holding her in their embrace, the water surrounding Beth began to thrash about like a miniature storm. There was a flurry of sudden activity and intense excitement, and then the waters fell calm once more. Heavy breathing and a gentle wave, to the stillness and thoughts, once more returning to her sensual and luxurious surroundings, and a feeling of utter release on Beth's face. As warmth and comfort took control once more, Beth decided to get dressed and not leave Isaac in limbo any longer.

She ran to the bedroom with her shaky legs from the extreme intensity of the last hour. Frantically going through her case, she was thinking out loud, "Oh no, not this one or that skirt, with my blue floor shirt. Oh, I know, my white shirt and black skirt with black tights and flat shoes." Then sitting in front of the mirror brushing her thick, dark brown, wavy hair, she applied a bit of lipstick and eyeliner. She was ready. "No," she thought, "these shoes don't feel right. Where are my boots?" She clambered under the bed to find her shoes. Beth quickly did up the laces and she was finally ready.

A note from the night before lay on the carpet. It said, "I am in the Tudor suite, 4th floor. Isaac." Beth left her room and made her way down the corridor. As she approached the lift, she saw the door of a room opening. A man and a woman scurried out. The lady turned to Beth saying, "Oh, we will be out for a couple of hours, so you can make our room now. Thank you and goodbye." Giving Beth five pounds in her hands as a tip, she said, "For you darling."

Beth was fuming, but by the time she had composed herself, they had gone. "Oh well," Beth thought, "that's five pounds I didn't have, so I'll buy something nice and thank them later."

On reaching the 4th floor, Beth knocked on the door. It slowly opened, "Beth," the voice said.

Beth looked towards Isaac and replied, "Dr. Jekyll, I presume." His hair was standing as if he had been struck by the lightning. There was a five o'clock shadow on his face. His eyes were bloodshot and his clothes were all bundled up in a crumpled mess. "Well, are you going to let me in?" Beth gestured.

"Oh, of course, but I'm not in a presentable state. Please excuse me."

"Yes, well, you should have seen me this morning." Beth replied with a smile and continued, "Right Isaac, you go get yourself a shower and a shave and I can order some breakfast for us. Do they have room service here?"

"Of course they do," laughed Isaac.

"Don't laugh at me!" Beth snarled. "You've got a lot of explaining to do."

"Yes of course," Isaac replied sheepishly. "I will see you shortly."

Beth walked to the cathedral shaped windows, spanning the whole view of Isaac's living room area and gazed at the city below - traffic as far as the eye could see, hustle and bustle like ants scurrying about. Beth opened a window, just enough so that she could hear the sounds. There were traffic noises, sirens, music, and an array of voices emanating from the streets below. She quickly pulled the window shut; the noise was unbearable to Beth as she ran a collage of pictures of Corngurn in her mind - the peace and quiet and the surreal beauty for everyone to behold. It suddenly occurred to her that Isaac might want to live here and for a moment she was filled with dread at that very thought. Her thoughts were interrupted by a knock at the door. "Come in," Beth replied. A very well-dressed porter wheeled a trolley draped in white linen, flowers at the center and an assortment of silver dome trays dishes and dishes, platters and cutlery. "Where would like me to set it up, madam?" the well-dressed man asked.

"On the table please, if you don't mind," Beth nervously answered.

"It will be my pleasure madam," he replied. "Are you here on business or holiday, miss?"

"A bit of both I fear, I don't really know," she said with a look of confusion on her face.

"Very well madam. Will there be anything else you require?"

Beth wondered for a moment what she was supposed to say. "Thank you…no, go… goodbye." The porter made a hasty departure from the room with a look of surprise on his face. Beth just felt embarrassed by her reply. "What an idiot!" she thought.

Just then the bathroom door opened. There stood Isaac in his big white hotel dressing gown. "Did I hear the porter with the breakfast? I am starving," he said. As he made his way to the table, he said, "Come on Beth, dig in." So they both sat and engulfed the food before them. Both of them had not eaten the day before as they didn't have the appetite with Isaac's revelations, Beth's feelings of being betrayed, an argument and finally Beth leaving him confused and sad. A day that should have been filled with joy had turned to misery, but the sun had risen once more. It was a new day and hope again beckoned towards a happier outcome. Beth and Isaac were quiet as they ate.

"Beth, would it be a good time now to talk more about what I started yesterday?" Isaac apprehensively asked.

"Yes, tell me all and leave nothing out," Beth sternly replied, so Isaac began.

He told her the truth, he shared everything with Beth - his suspicions, his thoughts, his life, the Van Horns, and his family. Beth sat quietly, listening to everything and realised that Isaac had seen his fair share of disappointment in his life. At one time he may have been a terrible man, but he had come out of the other side a different person. This, for Beth, was not the man she knew. The man Beth fell for was sincere, respectful, passionate, smiled and laughed a lot and above all he loved her, as she loved him with all of her heart and with that the rest would follow. Isaac continued. Beth looked up and just said, "Isaac I love you. I don't want to hear any more. I have faith in you. My heart now belongs to you. The talking is over and now we need to get on with living our lives together." Beth stood up from the breakfast table, kissed Isaac on the forehead, and whispered in his ear, "Five minutes love and I will see you in the bedroom."

CHAPTER TWELVE

Confrontation

B ETH LAY BACK ON THE large ornate bed, almost swimming in the silken sheets, which caressed her body, outlining each and every curve. Crease after crease unfolded the body of a goddess entwined in form with sensuality. Changing and alive with every movement, she had never in her life experienced this feeling of ecstasy. She beckoned to Isaac to come closer. However, he could not move as this unassuming, quiet, reserved and naive woman was now overwhelmed with ecstasy as if she has been taken to another realm, where all her inhibitions were for the first time set free. Isaac became entranced by what was unfolding before his eyes. His heart started to quicken, a hot warm glow engulfed him and an uncontrollable shaking in his whole body submerged his very being. In all his life, he had never dreamed of a goddess but there she lay before him, the one he loved, his manhood fighting to control this shivering mess of a man. "Isaac, come to me," beckoned Beth. "Hold me, my love, I want to feel you beside me," she said, her eyes aglow, her hair cascading and entwining with the colours from the ocean of silk that engulfed her. Isaac stood before her. His robes dropped to the floor to reveal his muscular physique and his erectness unwavering and surging in life's blood. Impetuous for an awakening and thrust through to life's beginnings, Isaac almost flowed into the large ornate bed beside Beth. Putting his arms out, he gently brought her towards him in a tender embrace. Their warm bodies were intertwined in love's desires. Isaac and Beth kissed for the longest of times while running their hands over each other's bodies, exploring the sculptures like artists. They were getting more and more excited with every touch. It seemed as if this was the first time because it was nothing like they had experienced before. Isaac gently caressed Beth's moist valley of life, his fingers a flutter of excitement as he started to explore his way down Beth's body, pausing with sensual kisses, a warm breath and a taste of desire. Beth writhed beneath him, almost losing all control. Any inhibitions she had were long departed. As Isaac reached her valley of ecstasy, his mouth tasted the essence of his goddess. He entered her, while his fingers explored all the zones of excitement and flow. Beth's body was infused with explosions of excitement. She could barely contain herself, as Isaac once more came face to face with his love and with a single thrust they were conjoined as one. Time almost seemed to stop for that perfect moment, when their universes became as one and life began anew.

Isaac lay beside Beth, one arm pillowing her head, and the other cuddling her. He said, "There are no words for what I have felt. I love you very much and that's the only way I can explain it."

Beth smiled, her eyes wide open and she just quietly said, "I also love you, Isaac Montgomery." Then they gently fell asleep in each other's arms, while the miracle of life took hold. For such intensity and passion, a life would begin anew. This was the start of a story of unending love between two hearts that the universe has deemed to be together; two broken souls had become complete. After a couple of hours, Isaac woke up. He decided to go down to the coffee shop and get Beth a cappuccino that she really seemed to like the day before. By the time Isaac got back, Beth was up and dressed. She sat on the large reclining sofa, looking out over the city through the arches of glass. "Here you go my love, a hot cappuccino."

"Oh thank you, you lovely man, just what I needed. Sit down Isaac, I need to ask you something. You do know I love you, don't you? And all I want is to be with you, but it is not possible here in London. I love my home; the rolling mountains, the greenery, the quiet and peaceful village that I can feel safe in. It is Christmas with the snowfall and the teardrops that freeze on your face, you are transported to a winter land of beauty. I love to see my family around the table, singing on Christmas and happiness sounding out over the valley as everybody rejoices another year. No matter how bad things get, I always feel safe there."

Isaac listened intently and then replied, "This is what I want too. I have never known such happiness before. I didn't even think I was capable of loving anyone. I had reached crossroads in my life and happiness stalked my every waking moment, and then I met you. You give me meaning, you make me a better person. If I could spend the rest of my life with you in Corngurn, it would be enough for me," Isaac said proudly. "But, what I need to ask you is to give me a week to get my affairs in order and we will travel back to Corngurn together."

Beth had a concerned look on her face. For a moment she fell quiet and then replied, "A week? Take two if you need, but then say you will take me back home." A look of sadness appeared in her eyes.

"I will. I promise," Isaac said as he hugged Beth tenderly. "I love you." A few minutes went by as they both cuddled and looked out over the city. "Beth?" Isaac whispered.

"Yes?"

"Oh, I thought you were asleep. I hope you don't mind, I've booked a day for you and Penelope, my best friend's fiancé in the spa here at the hotel. Hopefully, a day of total indulgence and I would so like you to meet Pen. Later on, I thought we could go to dinner with them. If you don't feel ready, I can cancel."

"No, I think I'll cope," replied Beth. "Where will you be Isaac?"

"I'm going back to see my uncle. We're meeting at his club at 12:30. I need to know exactly what he thinks my role is at the firm. Also, I want him to know, how I see my life. Basically, I want out of the business and to be left alone to live my life. If my head comes back in a basket, you'll know how it went." He saw a look of fear and concern on Beth's face. "Don't worry! I'm just joking."

"Isaac, from what you have told me last night, be very careful. I know with all your bravado, it's not going to be that simple. I know you are not kidding and just trying to make me feel better, so all I'll say is take care."

Just then there was a knock at the door. It was Penelope. "Is Beth ready?" she asked.

"Oh sorry, we were talking and the time just got away from us. Please come in. Beth, this is Penelope."

"At last, I meet the woman who has taken the wind out of Isaac's sails," Pen smiled.

Beth smiled and replied, "We are going to have a great day together. Would you like a drink?"

"Isaac, make yourself scarce. Beth and I have a big day planned and we don't need a man spoiling it."

Isaac kissed Beth on the forehead. "I'll see you later."

***

"Isaac Montgomery to see Mr. Van Horn."

"Yes sir, he is expecting you. Please follow me." He was sitting in his leather big winged back chair with a cigar in one hand and a drink in the other. "Nice to see you, Isaac. Take a seat. Smithers, a glass of port for my guest. That is your poison, isn't it Isaac?"

"Not for me, thank you. Von, can we speak?"

"Fire away, I'll catch up Isaac."

"I want to know what exactly you expect of me."

"I expect you to do your duty."

"And what is that duty?"

"It is simple. You are to become a partner in Van Horns. This will make me and my late brother proud and eventually a new Van Horn will take the seat of power and will be called Isaac Van Horn."

"But what if that's not what I want?" Isaac pleaded.

"It is your right of succession. We are like a monarchy and you are next in line for the throne. The eldest son of the eldest brother, and that's the way it has always been."

"But there must be somebody else, more worthy than me. Somebody who wants this honour."

"No, you are the one. You have a great flair and insight into the stock market. You've shown over the years that you are hungry for the game. You left carnage in your wake, nobody got in your way, you are stronger than you know, and you will not walk away from this. The decision has been made by the board; I will stand down and you will take my place, ready to battle on the floor of the stock exchange. Billions and billions pass through our counting house every day. We are the guardians of all this wealth. Countries fall, governments crumble, but Van Horns get stronger. We control banks, we govern prices throughout the world. Our name means little to the average man on the street, but all the world leaders and financial houses fear the decisions we make each day in our board rooms all over the planet. This is bigger than one woman's love or how you feel about her. This has always been your destiny and yours alone."

"I do not want to be that man. I have chosen my life's path. I am overwhelmed that I have a new family that I didn't even know existed, but this life and everything about it now is against everything I want. I could have the world full of money but that wouldn't put its arms around me when I am feeling low or whisper in my ear the words 'I am here for you' or tell me simply 'I love you.' Money has no feeling, good or bad, when it's destroying a man's livelihood or when someone winning the lottery. It doesn't pick or choose, it's just money, the root of all evil, what men and women kill for, save for, pray for, and the greed of those, who pursue so vigorously. Nothing else matters, just money. Nobody can live without it but we have to constantly chase it. And in the process, we miss everything beautiful around us, from the sun rising in the morning to the moon rising at dusk. I don't want to be that person, I want to be free to follow my own path."

"Poppycock," Von replied. "I've never heard such a load of dribble in all my life. Whether we like it or not, we do what must be done. And for me, your road is clear. You don't walk away from this; you stand up like a man and accept your future and your life, while you still have a life."

Isaac sat quietly for a moment and then looked at Von, "I know the truth about Victor's accident. My mother told me on her deathbed,"

"Your mother knew nothing about Victor's death," Von angrily answered. "It was an accident."

"No, you're right. She just thought it was an accident, but from your response, it seems that you knew a lot more about it than you say."

"Victor was a fool! He wanted to leave the company for a woman, and that to a married one. Like you, he went on and on about love and getting away," Von bellowed. "But when a chairman of a company like Van Horn's brings scandal openly to our doors, our shares all over the world would have gone down. And even if it would have been by one percent, we would have lost billions overnight. And no, I didn't get my brother killed, but somebody on the board did. I know this to be true and his time is coming. As for your theory about money being the root of all evil, yes it is, but it is the life we were born into. The only way I can retire is by naming my successor, and I have chosen - it's you. So the truth is, Victor wanted out, but you are here to take over,"

"But why kill him?"

"The main reason was the money. Secondly, he didn't have the permission to do what he did. A scandal is frowned upon in the halls of power. Victor was a victim of his own success and had he done things a different way, he may still have been alive today."

"Then that is my question. How can I do things differently, so that I can walk away? He sought happiness and it was taken away from him. I cannot become a chairman of something, I don't believe in anymore, I will probably run the company badly because I have no conviction towards it. For me, it would have destroyed my only chance at happiness and I would end up hating it and destroying it in the process."

"The fact is that there has always been a Van Horn at the helm of this ship," Von gestured. "But over the years with recessions and bad investments, shares had to be sold to other people to keep Van Horns moving forward with contracts, stipulations, and other sorts of legalities. So, although we still own 52 per cent of our own company, it's the other 48 percent that runs it now and that isn't going to change. But, we as a family, will always have our interests watched over by our own, and that will someday fall to you."

"You say someday. Does that mean you're not retiring right now?" Isaac eagerly awaited the answer.

"No. I have another five years before I step down," Von explained, "and you take my place. But you have to be ready. When you would become known to the board, they would look at your past within the company. Otherwise, you would also become a victim like your father."

"What of all the other Van Horns?" Isaac questioned. Won't they able to step up? Your own son, Edgar?"

Von thought for a moment. "He is good at what he does, but you are the gifted one. This is why you are chosen. If you're with them, nothing will happen to you, if you go against them, you would be taken care of just like your father...my brother."

"And you wouldn't lift a finger to help me?" Isaac proclaimed.

"I have protected you all your life. I too have 24 hr protection; that's just the way it is in our line of business, but the truth is if they want you dead, it will probably come true. We do whatever needs to be done to assure our legacy. That is the way it has always been and always will be."

Isaac took a moment, calculating everything his uncle had told him. He was running different ideas through his mind, hoping to come up with an answer to his dilemma.

"Another drink, sir?" A voice asked.

"Yes Smithers, I will have another. Isaac?"

"Just a coffee, please."

"Well, my boy, what are you thinking? I can almost see those cogs churning in your mind."

"Well, I won't take over from you for five years, yes? So, for the next five years could I work for you from Scotland? If I could speak to you every day, and once a month I spend a week in London, would it be possible to follow everything from an office in Corngurn? I would be able to use my computer, access emails, and do everything that is needed to continue a successful business. Is it really necessary that I be in London?" Isaac questioned. "I could take conference calls, straight to the board room if required. Could we not make this work between us?"

"That, my boy, is something that we can work out. That way you would be able to have your cake and eat it; the best of both worlds. If only years ago, Victor had spoken to me like this, the outcome could have been so different. Between you and me, we will make this happen, but once I retire in 5 years' time, you will have to take your rightful place as the chairman of Van Horn's House of Money. And what you do then, will be upon your own head." While listening to Isaac, Von was carefully assessing his replies. He was aware that if he didn't tread carefully, he would not get the desired result. Von listened and from time to time nodded his head in agreement at the flow of possibilities being presented to him. Von knew the truth and thought, "You live in your fantasy world and suggest all you like. Because I would be the one who sculpts you into my new unstoppable money-making machine. Slowly your defences will fall and bitterness for the priers we serve will become hatred and resentment. You will do what you have to but the end result will be that Van Horns will be better and stronger than ever before. And the life you hope for yourself will be a distant memory that could have belonged to someone else, for that is not your destiny anymore. You will marry, perhaps have children, but not to a simple-minded peasant, who hails from God knows where." Isaac continued his itinerary of how things could be. Von just sat with a drink in one hand, and a cigar in the other, deciding in his own mind how it was going to play out. "Von," Isaac said with a concerned look on his face.

"Sorry, yes?"

"I thought you were having a seizure; you were totally blank for a minute."

"I'm sorry my boy. So much is on my mind at the moment, and the older you get the more you forget. Anyway, I'm back in the room now, Isaac." Von gently broached the subject of Beth. "I mean no disrespect to you, but do you really think marrying this poor naive girl from Scotland is the way forward for you? Please don't get angry, I'm just voicing an opinion to the reality of life in your circumstances. Currently, we can make the transition as fluid as possible, but as time moves forward, do you not see yourself having problems with two such alien backgrounds that Beth and you hail from?"

Isaac thought of the words Von had spoken to him and his reply was swift, "Generations ago, were the Van Horns, not themselves the peasant stock, as you call it? But I will tell you," Isaac snapped, "If I am forced to choose it will be Beth and to hell with Van Horns."

Von suddenly realised the implication of his words and quickly retracted them. "I'm sorry Isaac, I didn't mean it the way it came out. I was just concerned about your differences, but of course, I know you will find a way. I have faith in you and I'm sure Beth is as strong minded as you are. So again, please accept my apology and let's move on." Isaac regained his composure. However, at the back of his mind, he could see the sense in what Von had said. He thought, "Beth? Will she be able to cope with my life and a series of different possibilities? Because if she can't, I will give it all up for her."

"How long are you staying in London?" Von questioned.

"Till my mother's funeral on Friday, then I'll take a flight back on Saturday."

"Thursday then?" Von replied. "I want you to meet some of your extended family, you are now part of. I will send you the details of the venue."

"How many are there?"

"You will see my boy, just be there and bring Beth. I feel she is going to be family soon enough. Till Thursday then."

"Thank you for your help, Uncle Von."

"Get out. You're spoiling my leisure time with your formalities. You ingrate and take care of that woman of yours." Isaac walked away with a smile on his face, something that he had found hard of late. But now, he could see possibilities of living his life with Beth in Scotland and fulfilling his obligations to his uncle by one day running the family business. He thought, "I know this is a short term solution to my problem, but now I have 5 years to make a life and live it; to show Beth just how much I love her and I hope the rest will fall into place."

CHAPTER THIRTEEN

Dire straits

DINNER WITH PHIL AND PEN was the first time that Beth and Isaac had properly sat down with another couple for polite conversation and good food. Isaac thought "Pen was right I used to be just wrapped up in myself to notice anything or anybody that didn't interest me, but as silly as it sounds, I suddenly feel grown up. What a thing for a 30-year-old man to say!" They had a fantastic night and Pen arranged to take Beth shopping the following day. Isaac was going to finalise things with his Uncle Von. But for now, it was just Beth and Isaac's night. Isaac turned to Beth, "Would you like to go to a club and we can dance the night away?"

"No, thank you, Isaac. Let's just go back to the hotel. I didn't realise a day of pampering could be so tiring."

"Your wish is my command."

"Taxi," Isaac hailed. "The Connaught Hotel please."

When they got back to the hotel, Isaac opened the door to the room. Beth said, "I need to go to my room to get my things,"

"It's all been done, I called them earlier. I hope you don't mind."

"Isaac just kiss me and hold me. That's all I've wanted all day. Oh, and how did it go with your uncle today?" Beth asked. "I think it went very well." Isaac turned around to look at Beth, but she had soundly fallen asleep on the large sofa, overlooking the city through the big windows. Isaac carried her to the bedroom, laid her on the bed, took off her shoes and covered her with the top blanket. He slowly got into the bed himself and cradled her to sleep.

The next morning, Beth and Isaac went down for breakfast. Soon after, Penelope came to take Beth shopping, "Give me your credit card, Isaac," Pen gestured, "We are doing the whole works today, aren't we Beth?"

"If you say so," Beth replied. "I have some money…I've got nearly £100."

"That would just be the bus fare in London," Pen laughed.

"Isaac, are you sure? You don't have to buy me things."

"Beth you're priceless! Just go and have a nice day!" Isaac decided to book the tickets back to Scotland for Saturday mid-morning. He arranged everything. He was eager to leave the city and go back to Corngurn to have his love all to himself. Just then Isaac got a call. It was Howard. "I would like to see you, can you come back to the house? We have things to talk about."

"Yes, I think I know what it is you want to discuss. I will be there within an hour, so if you're bored, start packing." Six months ago, Isaac would have thrown him out in one day and thought nothing of it, but now he just felt bad. He thought, "I know he has money, so he won't be destitute, but there are perhaps certain things that I don't know about." An hour later Isaac arrived at Montgomery Manor. Simpson opened the door, and Isaac walked straight to the study. "Howard."

"Isaac." Howard continued "Where to start?"

"How about the way you treated my mother?" Isaac snarled. Howard's stiff upper lip and his control started to evaporate before him. He broke down almost unravelling before Isaac's eyes. This man had only days before been so rude and arrogant. Now a shell of his former self, it was Isaac who seemed to have a total disregard for him. It was as if he had to break him and demoralise him.

"Are you ok sir?" Simpson asked.

"Get the man a drink please."

Howard bowed his head, with one hand on the fireplace, as if it was all that was holding him up. Simpson gave his master a drink. "Simpson, would you leave us for a while. We have things to talk about."

"Yes sir, just ring if you need me."

"Thank you, Simpson," Howard replied.

"Is this all about the house?" Isaac asked.

Howard's head lifted. "I don't give a damn about this house; it is empty to me now, bricks and mortar and nothing else. A prison that had held your mother and me together."

"Then why didn't you leave years ago?" Isaac asked.

"You really don't understand, do you? I loved your mother more than life itself, and I lost her the day your father Victor was killed. Yes, everything about me your mother told you was true. In the early days, I was overwhelmed with the attention and I reveled in it. I had a mistress, occasional relationships; I was a complete and utter bastard and in my stupidity, I thought I wasn't hurting anybody. I kept it away from home, so I thought it was ok. Then one day after an argument with your mother, she said she despised me and wanted me out of her life. In my arrogance, I could not believe what she was saying to me. The trouble was I really did love your mother. I promised I would change, become a one-woman man. I would devote myself to her, but of course, it was too late, the damage had been done, and I couldn't turn the clock back. If I could have, in that very instant, I would have done it. Your mother had fallen out of love with me and I had fallen back in love with her. For years after, we did our own things and we put up a good front for the outside world. I never again sought the affections of another. I was determined to make your mother fall in love with me again, but my betrayals had been the ultimate straw and although she was tolerant with me, I would never ever win her back. Then, on that fateful night, I went to her bedroom and she was packing her and the children's cases. She was leaving me for Victor and he was on his way. As you already know, Victor never made it. Once Isabel found out what had happened, I think a piece of her died that night, and that was the day I lost her forever. It was nearly five months before I even knew she was pregnant. After you were born, she had a complete mental breakdown and it was nearly two years in hospital before I got her back home. I admit that I never wanted you. You just reminded me of what I had lost, but I promised your mother you would never go without anything if she would let you go and stay with me. Well, she did stay, but she never let go of the memory of you. So, we still went through the motions, attending all the functions and to the outside world we were happily married, but once the doors closed for the outside world, we became strangers in a house full of memories. When I first met your mother, she was so vibrant and naïve. Her eyes saw the world around her as a happy place; she was full of life and she loved me unconditionally and supported everything I wanted to do. And the reality is, I threw that special gift away without a second thought. But when I tried to get that back, it was too late and now all that's left is a bitter old man with nothing to live for. For me this is just a rotting house; any goodness that was left has died with your mother's last breath and now I plan to follow her even into death. I cannot live without her."

By now Howard was on the floor.

Isaac shouted, "What have you done?" Howard stumbled forward. Isaac rang the bell quickly. Simpson appeared. "Call an ambulance quickly, I think he has taken something!"

"Just let me die, I don't want to live alone." Howard bellowed.

Isaac picked him up, tried to make him move around, but he was just a dead weight in his arms. "Stay awake!" he shouted. "Wake up Howard!" He slapped his face but he just seemed to be willing himself to death. Then, suddenly, he stopped breathing. Isaac pounded on his chest and used CPR on him, something that he had seen once before, and Howard began to come around just a little. "Simpson, Simpson!" Isaac shouted.

"I'm here sir."

"How long for the ambulance?"

"They're on their way, sir."

Five or ten minutes later, two paramedics rushed into the room. "Ok sir out of the way, we'll take over from here." After a little while, they managed to stabilise him. "Right, we'll take him to the hospital."

"Will he be alright?" Isaac questioned.

"It's too early to say anything yet. Once we get to the hospital, they will be able to tell you more."

"Do you know what he might have taken?" Luckily, Simpson had checked his medicine cabinet and found an empty bottle of anti-depressants that he had taken. "That will help," the paramedic said, "They will be able to give him the right treatment once we get him there."

"Simpson!" Isaac shouted. "Go with him. I will see you there." Running through Isaac's mind was the fact that only two days before he had nearly killed this man for being such an absolute bastard and now he was fighting to keep him alive. How our lives twist and turn; we never know what will happen next. For a minute, everything seemed so clear and the next it was all gone to shit. Isaac told the staff that their master had been taken ill and Mr. Simpson had gone with him to the hospital. They were to just carry on as normal and Simpson would tell them what was happening when he gets back.

By the time Isaac arrived at the hospital, Simpson was sitting at the reception, a grim look on his face. "How is he, Simpson?"

"He died, sir. Despite all their efforts, he just slipped away. He really didn't want to live without your mother."

"You knew who I was?"

"Yes, sir. I worked for your family when you were born."

"He really did love my mother, didn't he?"

"Yes sir, he did. But she never forgave him and that's what he couldn't live with. He became a tormented man throughout his time in this world for throwing away the best thing he had – your mother." He added, "I know it's probably insensitive at the moment sir, but what will happen to the house and the staff? They would want to know."

"I have no plans as such, there are legalities that I have to look into. I know my mother left me the house. Oh, and yes, will you tell Helen and Edward of their father's death? They have lost their mother and father, all in one week."

"Would it not be better coming from you, sir?"

"No, I haven't seen them in 22 years or so. They wouldn't even know me if I passed them on the street."

"As you wish sir," Simpson replied.

"I have no doubt we will talk at the funeral for my mother on Friday," Isaac said. "Have you arranged anything back at the house?"

"No sir, but I will."

"Thank you, Simpson." Just then Beth called. "I'm back now at the hotel. Where are you?"

"I will be back soon."

"Hurry up Isaac. I have so much to show you and tell you about my day." Beth was excited.

"Yes, Beth. I will be there soon. I love you, and I will never let you go."

"Well, I love you too you idiot. See you soon. Bye."

When Isaac eventually arrived back at the hotel after taking Simpson back to the house, he wanted to tell Beth about his day. But she was very happy, and for now, he didn't want to take that away from her. Beth talked over dinner about the places she had been the things she had bought and the strange and weird places Pen had taken her to. After dinner, they went back to their room. They were barely at the door and they were all over each other. They made love for what seemed like hours. She had dropped all her inhibitions and her modesty. She just wanted him as he wanted her. It was ecstasy in its purest form. As Isaac watched her sleep, still holding his hand, he thought that he had so much to tell her. The way his life seemed to be going of late, it would be better for her to run a mile. He hadn't even had a chance to tell her of his meeting with his uncle and what is expected of him in the next five years. But he knew that above all, he had to tell her the truth because she would expect nothing else. He had lied to her once, and that was once too many.

***

The next morning Isaac had the breakfast sent up to the room. He walked into the bedroom, woke Beth and put the tray on her lap with a single red rose. He gave her a kiss and said, "I need to tell you some things that have happened over the last couple of days." He told her about the meeting with his uncle and what had been decided. He also shared the details of his meeting with Howard and the results of that - how he had taken his own life because he could not live without Isaac's mother. Beth now knew everything. Isaac had nothing more to hide.

Beth said, "I don't pretend to understand this life you find yourself in, but I can certainly understand why you left it and why when you first met me, you pretended to be someone else."

"I have made a deal with my uncle and I will honour it, but we will live in Corngurn. And there is one other thing I need to ask." Isaac dropped to one knee. "Will you marry me Beth McCoogan?"

"With all my heart, Isaac Montgomery!"

"Oh, I love you!" They held each other in that one perfect moment, where they had committed themselves to each other. "Can we get married in Corngurn?" Beth asked.

"We can marry anywhere you want to."

"I am so happy Isaac! I must call my family and tell them the news. Well, when will we go home?"

"Saturday afternoon, it's all booked."

"Oh, I love you…I love you…I love you!" Beth shouted at the top of her voice. "You've made me so happy." For Isaac, this was the feeling of being complete. He never dreamed that when he went to Scotland, he would find what was missing in his life. He felt with her beside him, he could face anything that life throws at him. Unfortunately, it was probably a bit premature to say something like that. But for now she had said yes and that made him the happiest man in the world. Later that day, they met Isaac's extended Van Horn family. It was like a who's who of the rich and famous. Von wasn't kidding when he said to meet the family - there were police, bodyguards and private security everywhere. They were all there to guard the families, who were there to meet Beth and Isaac in his role as the future president of Van Horns' empire. The main subject of the night was the highest job any Van Horn could aspire to and as the new deputy president, Isaac was on his way. Victor's son would steer the ship to prosperity for the Van Horn Empire. Aunties, uncles, cousins, close friends, the board, celebrities, they shook hands with both of them. Isaac got patted on the back so many times during the night that he was sure he would have a handprint etched on his back forever. But, all in all, it was a fantastic night. By the time they got back to the hotel room, they were exhausted and went straight to bed. It was the funeral of Isaac's mother the next day and he would come face to face with his half-brother and sister once more. Isaac was just waiting for Saturday when we would fly back to the peaceful Scotland, his new home.

The following day, Isaac arrived early at the church and walked up the long footpath towards the church doors, which was full of people from all walks of life. Isabel had done so much during her life, she had been good to so many people with her charity work that she was involved in. It was ironical that she had done so much for so many, but could never help herself. The ceremony went quite well. People praised her and spoke of her tireless efforts to help many with her different projects. She truly was a light to the outside world and would be missed. Then one woman stood up and Isaac thought, "That face seems familiar. She looks so much like Mom." It had to be Helen. She started her eulogy; barely a sentence was out when she broke into tears. A tall distinguished kind of man walked up and cuddled her and started to read. It must have been Edmond; he had the look of Howard about him. It was unbelievable that Isaac had not seen them for more than 20 years. But they were his half-brother and sister. Isaac grabbed Beth's hand and held it tightly. "What is it, Isaac?"

"Ghosts from the past," he replied. "That I finally must meet face to face and see what sort of reaction I get." They all stood by the graveside, peering into this wet damp hole, the final resting place of Isaac's mother. Slowly, everyone began to leave and a long procession of vehicles headed off towards Montgomery Manor for the wake. As they walked through the large oak doors, Helen and Edward were standing there thanking all the people who had attended their mom's funeral. Isaac put his hand out and Helen shook it and said, "Thank you for coming."

I said, "You don't remember me, do you?"

"I'm sorry," she said. "There are so many here today."

"I'm Isaac."

Edward heard this. His head turned quite quickly. He said, "Isaac? Our long lost brother?"

"Yes," Isaac replied. Edward grabbed him, making him think that he was going to squeeze him to death, but he just hugged him and Helen put her arms around them both. Isaac couldn't believe it; they were actually overwhelmed to see him.

Helen said, "After all the people have gone, we must talk. It's so good to see you after all these years. Say you'll stay until the end."

"Of course I will. It will be good to catch up and talk."

"Till later then," Helen smiled. After that, Beth and Isaac just mingled from one group to another. Nobody knew who he was and he didn't see it necessary to introduce himself. They just said they were friends of the family. Helen had reached earlier that morning and had arranged the staff and the caterers. She also spoke to Simpson about the arrangements. Simpson had not divulged that Isaac had been with Howard when he died the day before. He thought it was best if Isaac explained it to them himself. Isaac thanked Simpson for his discretion in this matter. The day seemed to drag on and people left very slowly. Meanwhile, Beth and Isaac retired to the study. Isaac told Simpson that when Edward or Helen ask for him, he should inform them that he is waiting for them here.

"I will tell them, sir," Simpson replied.

"How are you feeling?" asked Beth.

"I just don't know what to say to them," Isaac replied.

"You must tell them about what your mother told you and the reason Howard took his own life. They didn't see him at the end but you did, so they're going to have questions."

"You know in so many ways, I wish I had never come back to this place. It's all such a mess of truths and half-truths, revelations and lies. Do you think we should just go?"

"Isaac, you know you won't do that."

"I know, it was just wishful thinking."

Just then Helen and Edward appeared at the door. They all hugged briefly again. "Oh, this is Beth, my fiancé." With pleasantries out the way, they all sat and discussed the usual questions - "So, you saw Mom and you spoke to her before she died? That's good. How have you been over the last few years?" The general summation of their lives continued until they got to the most serious side of the conversation. "If you don't mind me asking, why have you and Edward never tried to get in touch with me? It's not as if I've been in hiding," Isaac asked.

The room fell silent for a moment.

"Well, Dad said you wanted nothing to do with us. He said you told him that we were nothing in your life and that's the way you wanted it to stay." Edward finally replied.

Isaac thought for a moment and then said, "Well that answers that question. He also told me the same - that the two of you wanted nothing to do with me because I was Mom's dirty little secret and a scandal that had to be kept away from the public eye. I also noticed the portrait in the hall sans me," Isaac said angrily.

Helen turned to Isaac. "You mean you never had any form of relationship with our father?"

"No, he had nothing to do with me, and he wouldn't even let my mother communicate with me in any form, until she was dying and on her death bed. That was when she offered me many answers that I was seeking all my life," Isaac explained. "She told me the truth in the brief time she was left with." Beth, by this time, was squeezing Isaac's arm tenderly, as her eyes began to fill with tears. They were all shocked; they knew nothing of who their mother had the affair with or the fact that she planned to leave with him and take them all with her. They were also unaware that Isaac was the result of their mother's affair.

"We knew the mother was pregnant," Edward answered. "But we thought you were Dad's." When we asked about you, he told us that you were stillborn and that's why Mom had her breakdown. He also said that we must not talk about it when we are with Mom because she was so very frail and it could send her into a depression. It was a few years later that we found out the truth from Mom. When we confronted our father, he told us you wanted nothing to do with us and we should not pursue the matter, because it would open up too many old wounds that could break our family apart. And even though we would have liked to meet you, we thought we would be going against our father's wishes. Then the time went by and the life got busier and there just didn't seem any time anymore. I'm so sorry Isaac, it's not your fault and I can see that now."

Helen added, "This is all true. It became the same for me."

Isaac looked at Helen, a broken smile on his face. "I too had a hole in my life that needed to be filled," Isaac replied." You may not want to hear this, but a few days ago I had it out with Howard before I went to speak with Mom." Isaac told them the exact conversation they had. He also said that he eventually grabbed Howard by the throat and nearly killed him. He then informed them about the previous day and that he tried everything to save him, but he died shortly after. A silence fell upon the conversation, and their faces dropped. Helen without a word stood up and walked towards the door. Edward followed slowly behind her. They walked away, closing the door behind them. Isaac looked at Beth, "Now I have told them the truth, has it just not made the things ten times worse?"

Beth gently caressed Isaacs's hair and replied, "You have told them the truth, withholding nothing. If they cannot see how their father treated you and the things he had said, then they are not the people I thought they were."

"You know Beth, life with me is going to be very complicated over the next few years. But know one thing, I will always love you and you will always be my number one priority."

Beth held him. That warmth and a soft smile on her face were all Isaac needed. He felt as long as he had her beside him, he could take anything.

Simpson brought a tray of sandwiches and a drink. "Are my brother and sister coming back Simpson, do you know?"

"I'm afraid they've left sir," Simpson replied. "But Lady Helen left this note. I was to give to you."

"Did they ask you anything?"

"They had a number of questions for me sir, as they were leaving. I told them how you had desperately tried to save Mr. Howard's life when he had stopped breathing but he later died on his way to the hospital and how he hadn't wanted to live without his mistress. They were very upset by this and Master Edward said they needed to go and talk."

"Thank you for your honesty, Simpson."

Simpson bowed his head. "If there isn't anything else sir, I will retire for the night. I have had the guest rooms made up, should you decide to stay, and housekeeping will be at your disposal."

"Goodnight Simpson,"

"Goodnight Master Isaac, Mistress Beth."

Isaac turned to Beth, "Would you like a tour of this house. To be honest, it will be an experience for me too. I was too young when I left this place, I can remember nothing of it, but first, I must read Helen's note." Isaac pondered for a minute while holding the paper in his hand.

The note read, "Dear Isaac, I am sorry for our untimely departure, but there are things I need to get clear in my own mind before we meet again. We knew nothing about a lot of things that you have told us. Please give us some time to come to terms with all that has happened and I will call you soon. Helen and Edward."

"You know Beth, I suddenly don't really want to look around this place, not at this moment anyway. Let's go back to the hotel, have a nice meal and an early night. We've got a plane to catch tomorrow and hopefully, I can finally find some peace from all this."

"What will you do about the house?" Beth asked.

"I will instruct my lawyers to deal with it now and if I have to fly back next week, so be it."

"I just want a couple of days of normal routine to re-charge myself and take everything as it comes. It has been one hell of a week."

Beth replied, "I can think of some much stronger words than that."

"Why Beth, you fishwife."

"It is part of my charm," she smiled. As they drove away from Montgomery Manor, Isaac caught the house in his rear view mirror. It looked like a dark spooky cold place; the lights were out, the wind and the rain pummelled down upon it as if washing away the anguish and despair of the lives that are now gone. He couldn't help thinking that if he had not come, things would have been different. But then he thought, "No, my mother would have died from her illness and Howard would have seen to that and he would have followed her close behind and I would never have got the answers to the questions that haunted me. And now I would like to build a relationship with my brother and sister, but only time will answer if that is possible."

The next day Beth and Isaac woke up, washed and got dressed. They went straight down for breakfast. A few hours later, they were ready to leave. Isaac had his car brought around and started to put the cases in the car. Beth now had one more case after her shopping spree with Pen. He quickly walked into the hotel to pay his bill, so that they could leave. Suddenly a voice called, "Good morning Mr. Montgomery." He turned to see a stranger in a Saville Row suit. He had exquisite taste. "I'm sorry, have we met before?" Isaac asked.

"No," the man replied. "But I thought I would introduce myself. I am Ludvic Clouse. I am a board member at Van Horns. I believe we should talk."

"I'm sorry Mr. Clouse. I do know of you, but I am late for a flight at the moment. So, I have no time to spare, but I will be back in London next week sometime. Please leave a message with my secretary and she will make an appointment for us to meet."

"I will let you go," Clouse replied, "But believe me, when I have something to say, people listen or they face the consequences. Do we understand each other, Mr. Montgomery? When you get back to Scotland, call your uncle and ask him about me and then re-think your attitude."

Isaac replied, "I'm sorry. As I said I am in a hurry but make sure of one thing, I don't like to be threatened. We will revisit this at your convenience."

Clouse started to walk away with a few parting words. "Don't make it too long Mr. Montgomery."

A few hours later, they arrived in Glasgow and were picked up the hire car that was to take them to Corngurn. Both of them felt good to be back. Isaac felt like this was his birthplace, instead of the reality of his life. Ten miles from Corngurn, they were stopped at road works, and a worker tapped on the window.

"Yes, can I help you?" Isaac gestured. He looked Isaac straight into the eyes and said, "Mr. Clouse asked me to tell you to have a nice day." Then he walked away. Isaac knew what that message meant.

When they finally got back to the village, Isaac took Beth straight back to her parents' farm, and then returned to the last house on the right. He thought he should call his Uncle Von about this Ludvic Clouse right away. He had stepped over the line. When Isaac got back to the house, Summer had cleaned up and had done some shopping for him. Jacamo just looked at him and went back to sleep in front of the fire. Isaac called his uncle and told him about his meeting with Clouse and the interrupted journey back to Corngurn.

"What is his problem?" Von replied, "I know about Clouse coming to see you."

"Well, why didn't you tell me?" Isaac expressed angrily. "What about the road works?"

"Yes, I know," Von replied.

"How do you know unless he told you?" asked Isaac.

"Your watcher told me."

"I didn't see anyone," Isaac replied.

"That's the whole point, Isaac. You'll just know he's there and he will protect you with his life. The profession you are in now can be a dangerous place and we always look after our own. Extra security has been sent to you; just know that they are there. I will speak to Mr. Clouse in the morning. The last thing he should want is to create a rift between us."

"What do you mean anyway about this profession I'm in?" Isaac questioned.

"Don't be so naive, money and the want of money are what makes men do the evilest things. No matter how much they have, they still want that penny in your pocket. Some people see nothing but money and that is their life. Ludvic Clouse wants to be the head of Van Horns, the president. But unless he can buy five more shares of the company and get the backing of the board, it belongs to the Van Horns. I will see that he never gets what he craves."

"But why me? I have no shares in the company," Isaac said.

"Yes, you do. You have Victor's shares. They went to you on your 30th birthday. You now own 26 per cent of Van Horns' empire. I own the other 26 percent, which is our 52 per cent. You really haven't grasped just what it is you are part of."

"What about this Clouse fellow? How many shares does he have?"

"He only has 5 percent. Altogether, there are nine members with 5 percent and one with 3 per cent share. All hail from various conglomerates from all across the world. When you come back to London next week, I will make everything clear and your final training will begin. I promised you five years," Von continued "and as long as nothing happens in that time you will get those years. But once I retire, everything will change. So, you need to make that beautiful woman of yours know what your life will become. The Isaac I knew would have grabbed it with both hands six months ago, but now I sometimes don't see that man in you anymore. But you must find a way to make this work. You are a brilliant stockbroker, you see what others don't, and you on so many occasions have just baffled the market with your premonitions. You have the Von Horn trait for markets, and you are always one step ahead of the competition. You shouldn't lose a gift like that; you must enhance it. And you've got time over the next few years before you become head of the corporation. But always be aware of your competition, your opponents, for if they find a weakness, they will make a move on you and try to discredit you. You will have your good days and your bad, but you must always be on the top of your game."

"Right Uncle Von. I really need to get things set up here. I will see you next Tuesday. Thanks for the talk. I'm sure as I mull it over, I will get a better understanding."

Shortly after, Beth returned home and they settled in for the night. Isaac told her nothing about what their lives may become, because, in his own mind, he had five years to change the situation– well that's what he thought. He pondered, "I will have to find a way. I feel that I have now been tied to something that will one day control my very existence. In a lot of ways, I will once again have to become the old Isaac, who was hungry, cruel, and ambitious. But, I will always have two sides of my life - my family and my business; and they must never clash. What I want more than anything is Beth and a loving home. But, I am aware that I would be forced to lead a life that would compel me to become ruthless, suspecting and distrustful. I must train myself to lead one life with two faces. But for now, I have a relationship to work on with a woman, who I love dearly. I will get married, have children, and settle in Corngurn, but I would also honour my commitments to Van Horns. We will find a nice home to live in and do all the things that a family does. At the same time, I would run this company to the best of my ability, till the day I step down and finally be free.

It all sounded like a well laid out plan, but the truth for Isaac Montgomery was going to get a lot different from what he expected. He had not grasped the enormity of the task ahead. He wanted to have children and a peaceful life with Beth, but he had still not realised the complications that he would soon encounter.

The End

EPILOGUE

There would be attempts on Isaac's and his family's life; he would have to go into hiding, when his half-brother and sister would get to know about his mother's will. Though, on the day of the funeral they pretended that they wanted to be a part of his life, but there were more sinister games afoot. People would discredit him, there would be scandal and links will be made. Read as Isaac fights for everything he holds dear, as the world around him tries to systematically snatch it from him. His story is a long way from being over. In many ways, it's only just the beginning; like the best-laid plans of men and mice. This would be a fight he would have to win as his life and of those around him may soon be the victims of his legacy. There would come a time, when he would have to completely disassociate himself from his family to keep them safe. His story will continue…

Lightning Source UK Ltd.
Milton Keynes UK
UKOW01f0613060117
291482UK00001B/68/P

9 781524 668150